CW00496358

PAPER FORESTS

Also by
TEGAN ANDERSON

Beauty in the Breakdown

Paper Forests

PAPER FORESTS

TEGAN ANDERSON

Little Oaks

First published in Great Britain by
Little Oaks Independent Publishing

Text © 2023 Tegan Anderson
Cover illustration © 2023 Ksenia Kholom'yeva
Book design © 2023 Tegan Anderson

1 3 5 7 9 10 8 6 4 2

A CIP catalogue record for this book is available from the
British Library.

Hardcover:
Paperback:

Independently published

www.tandewrites.com

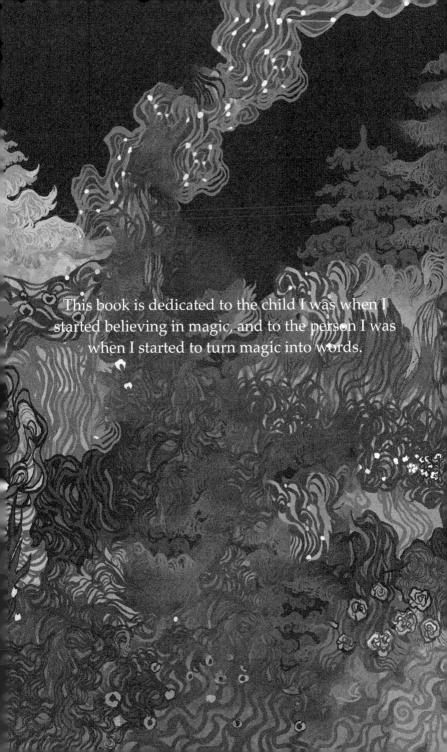

This book is dedicated to the child I was when I started believing in magic, and to the person I was when I started to turn magic into words.

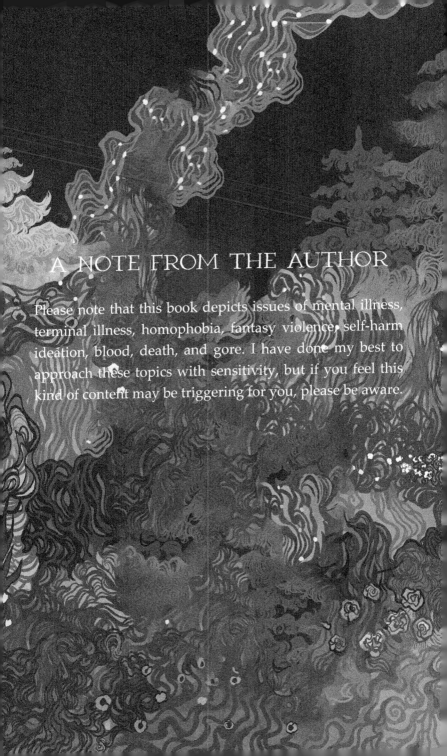

A NOTE FROM THE AUTHOR

Please note that this book depicts issues of mental illness, terminal illness, homophobia, fantasy violence, self-harm ideation, blood, death, and gore. I have done my best to approach these topics with sensitivity, but if you feel this kind of content may be triggering for you, please be aware.

PROLOGUE

In a counselling room with a circle of chairs, you would expect to find a group of teenagers. They would have empty eyes and slumped postures and minds that told them they were immune to the influence of society. However, those influences would be the reason they were in that room in the first place.

Now, the room is full of adults, holding on to each other as their final shreds of hope flicker before them.

"We'll go around the circle one by one," says a man who stands at the edge of the circle, scratching at the stubble across his cheeks. "Introduce yourself and tell us a little about why you're here, as much as you're comfortable sharing. Remember, we're here to support each other, not to block each other out."

The first person to stand is a woman, likely in her late forties or early fifties but looking many years past her age. She has the delicate features of a porcelain doll, but her tears smear her carefully applied makeup and her skin looks many sizes too big for her skinny frame. She smells like a cheap but strong floral perfume. There's a man beside her with an untrimmed moustache and a fuller figure from comfort eating. He doesn't stand.

"I'm Caroline Harwood. This is my husband, Michael. My son...*Our* son...His name is Oliver. He's in a coma. He's only seventeen."

Her hands shake as she talks, but her voice doesn't falter. Her words sound rehearsed, almost as if she's been repeating the same story over and over again to other counsellors, private therapists, or old friends who visit and ask where her eldest son is that day. The man beside her reaches up and holds one of her hands in both of his, bringing her knuckles up to his lips.

"He overdosed on heroin a few weeks ago and it

surprised the doctors that he made it. He's been on life support ever since. We're praying for the best, but it isn't looking promising."

A few tears leak out of her eyes as she sinks back into her chair, not uttering another word for the rest of the session.

The counsellor continues around the circle, all wet cheeks and hollow eyes blurring into one figure, looking like despair personified.

A young man is representing a little girl named Gracie. She was critically injured at age seven—along with her mother—in a car accident where he was driving. An elderly couple speaks about their grandson, Ansel, only fourteen years old. They weep until they remove their glasses and pull out tattered handkerchiefs. A middle-aged man and woman, who don't make eye contact or acknowledge each other's presence besides interrupting each other, talk about their son, August. He is a terminal cancer patient approaching the end of his life expectancy.

After allowing each child to be spoken about

for a few minutes, the counsellor steps in, sensing that the adults are becoming too distraught or too uncomfortable to continue. He stands in the centre of the circle and cracks his knuckles.

"One thing that you all have in common is that you have a child who is on the verge of being taken away from you, whether it is by a natural illness or something that could've been prevented. You mustn't worry, for they have been placed in the best hands and there are people who are trying their best to look after them."

The adults in the circle lean in, desperate to hear anything that could ease their pain, even if it's just a story woven for their own comfort. In this situation, it is a story, although there is some truth behind every word.

"While your children and grandchildren are away, I like to think that they're visiting a fantastic place, somewhere where they aren't restrained by an illness or held back by their own emotions. I like to believe that they're in a place called the Paper Forest, where there is nothing but health and happiness to greet them."

ONE

O nce upon a time, I awoke in a strange place. It was clear that this place was not my home.

The sun hasn't risen when I sit up and rub at my bleary eyes, surrounded by an almost familiar cold darkness and the stale aroma of dirt. Trees tower over me, almost one hundred feet tall, and the bark is as smooth as ice. The canopy of leaves is dark enough to be mistaken for black. Dried mud from the day before leaves smears across my clothing. The vegetation consists of only trees and sparse patches of dead grass. Everything around me looks different from yesterday; I think the world resets when I'm sleeping.

There may be no living grass, no flowers on the ground, but there are three sleeping people, all wrapped up in their dreams. They've been here for the past few days, the rise and fall of their chests being the only evidence that they were still alive. They are the only things which have remained the same since I woke up here, surrounded by unfamiliarity.

The sleepers lie in a triangle. There's a little girl, maybe seven or eight years old, with stubby brown braids and a cornflower blue raincoat. One of her hands clasps at her zipper while the other is curled into a fist by her face, her thumb tucked into her mouth. The other two sleepers are both teenage boys dressed in jeans and oversized band t-shirts. One is pale with hair like raven feathers and soft features. The other has a face made from sharp angles rather than curves, with skin like bronze marked with bruises and a mane of mahogany curls.

As much as I want to wake one of them, I resist the urge and walk through the trees instead, taking a mental note of the scenery so I can find my way back to where they rest. Waking one of them might change this world even further.

Seemingly endless, the Forest stretches out for what could be miles in each direction, every tree the same distance apart, organised as if they are soldiers about to step into battle. Everything is identical, but the spot where I woke up is the anomaly. There, the trees space out further and I slip on mud wherever I step, even though there is no sign of past rain or water nearby.

"Hello?"

I stop walking.

"Hello? Is someone there?"

It's the first sound I've heard in days other than my breathing and my shoes sticking in the mud.

"I can't see you. Can you come closer? I don't have my glasses." The raven-haired boy is sitting up, rubbing at his dirty face. His wide eyes and round cheeks don't match his scrawny frame. Although hunger and thirst no longer affect us here, his body looks as if he's been starved almost to death.

He squints in my direction, shielding his eyes with

his hands even though there's no sunlight to disrupt his view. I step into a patch of moonlight so he can see me better.

"My name is Ansel," he says hesitantly to fill the silence, and I realise I haven't responded to any of his calls.

"I'm Oliver." I scratch at my arms. The tiny dents and scabs that linger beneath my fingertips remind me of the last few moments of my life. The marks from the belt still haven't faded. They never will, not here. I'm frozen in the moment of my last breath. "Before you ask, I don't know where we are or how we got here. I woke up a few days ago. It changes every day."

"It changes?"

I nod. "The Forest changes everything but your clothes. On the first day, it was a rainforest. The second, it looked like something straight out of a Tim Burton film. Now," I pause while I look around, "it's just a muddy forest."

As I say this, Ansel peels himself from the ground, his clothes squelching as they pull away from the mud.

His face distorts in disgust as something cracks beneath his weight: his glasses. He curses, fumbles around for the remains, and then hurls them away as hard as he can. Here, there's nothing we can do to fix them.

We stand on opposite sides of the clearing, leaning against the trees and waiting as if we're wanting the other person to step forward and take charge, the one who will watch over the remaining two sleepers and find our way home. There's nothing we can say to each other, not until he realises why he's here. I know why I am.

The sun rises and sets again before another sleeper awakens. This time, it's the other boy, closer to my age than Ansel. He doesn't say anything. His paint-splattered hands tremble as he rubs at the bruises which decorate his skin, purple and blue roses against a brown canvas. One hand drifts towards his neck and he fumbles with the collar of his shirt as if he's looking for something. He drops the hand in defeat. All emotions evaporate from his face. His focus is somewhere behind me, as if I don't exist to him.

In another world, he could be beautiful.

In this world, he's a ragged thing, a boy tilting too close to monstrous.

I want to be afraid of him, but I'm not.

"What's your name?" Ansel asks. The boy does not move, but Ansel must close the distance between them to make out his features. He gets no reply, so he doesn't bother asking again. It's not like we're under a time constraint.

Time...I count seconds, then minutes, until I reach an hour. The sun appears over the horizon as I reach my target, almost as if the new world is listening to me. Today, the sunrise is beautiful, with orange-hued rays kissing candyfloss clouds and bringing warmth to the air. I don't have the chance to enjoy it.

The little girl wakes up as soon as the sun has fully risen. When she opens her eyes, she screams, a sound that seeps beneath my skin and is painfully wrong in such a childish voice.

I run towards her before my brain can register why. Ansel reaches her first, dropping to his knees and pulling her against his chest. She pushes him away and presses herself against the ground, each scream looking as if it is about to tear her body in two.

Nothing we say can console her, so the other boy and I keep our distance. I return to keeping note of our surroundings. A golden trail of sunlight illuminates a string of orange daisies sprouting up from the mud. They wind into the trees and out of sight.

Now that everyone is awake, we'll be able to start moving. There must be a way of figuring out where we are and how we can get home.

"It's okay," Ansel murmurs when the girl has calmed down enough to take a breath, wrapping his arms around her as she shakes. In this moment, he looks like an older brother trying to comfort her after a bad dream. "It's over now."

She looks up, not at Ansel, but into the canopy of the Forest above us. Her wide eyes lack the childish innocence that I've seen in my siblings.

"No, it's not," she whispers back. "It hasn't even begun."

We have been following the daisies for hours when the girl—Gracie, not Grace, she tells me firmly—runs up to me and grabs my hand. Her palms are cold and clammy, and I resist the urge to pull away. She quickens her pace to keep up with me; three of her steps are equal to one of mine.

"I feel strange," she announces after we've passed a few dozen trees. Her pink Velcro trainers stumble across protruding roots, so I slow down for her, casting an eye around to see where the others are. Ansel is striding confidently ahead of us, no longer disorientated by his broken glasses. The other boy is somewhere behind. I can't see him, but I can hear his heavy footfall crushing fallen twigs.

"What do you mean by 'strange'?" I ask, turning my attention back to Gracie. She stops walking and crosses her arms across her chest, crinkling the plastic of her raincoat. Her lips curl into a pout.

"I should be hungry. I haven't had my breakfast."

With that, she turns away and stomps ahead to catch up with Ansel. She's found comfort in him since this morning.

I understand what she's feeling. I woke up four days and I still haven't adjusted to the effects this new world has on me. My first instinct was to search for food and water, but I realised I didn't have an appetite by the time I found some. I carried berries around with me all day until the world reset and my pockets emptied. Hunger never found me. Neither did thirst.

As we walk, I hear snippets of Ansel and Gracie's conversation, occasionally broken by the other boy's movements like static.

"Have your parents told you the story of Hansel and Gretel?" Ansel asks. He's holding Gracie's hand and swings it with each step.

"No." I catch a glimpse of her screwing up her nose. "What's that?"

Even from this distance, I can see his body tense. He hesitates as if he didn't prepare for this scenario. "Hansel and Gretel were the children of a woodcutter.

One day, they were playing in the woods while their father was working, but they got lost."

"Oh." I hear the disappointment in Gracie's voice. If I were Ansel, I would've told her the authentic version of the story, the one with the parents selling the children and the witch fattening them up to eat.

"If you think about it, we're like Hansel and Gretel. We're lost in the woods and we can't find our parents."

"You're Hansel because your name sounds like Hansel."

He nods. "And you're Gretel."

Gracie stops in her tracks, tugging her hand back to herself. "No, I'm not," she insists. "Gretel is an ugly name."

Another hour passes before we decide to stop for a break. Exhaustion and fatigue don't seem to affect us anymore, but looking at nothing but trees for hours has bored Gracie and she needs time to rest her mind.

Time also works differently here: it goes faster. It was only a few hours ago when Gracie woke up just as the sun finished rising, but it's already dipping below the horizon. I wonder if we're in a northern country with short winter days and long nights, although the chill in the air isn't quite cold enough. It's like we've been snatched off the surface of the Earth and dumped into a world made just for us.

Gracie seems to grasp this concept a lot faster than the rest of us, maybe because she's still young enough to believe in stories of magic and fantasy worlds. She darts through the trees like a bird, spouting out random theories and eruptions of knowledge she must have invented during the first part of our journey.

"We're not the only living things here. There are prettier plants and animals and people if we keep walking." She takes off her coat and ties the sleeves in a knot around her shoulders like a cape. "We're going to catch up to everyone else soon and we'll all be together. We have to be together so we can be safe." She runs into gaps between the trees, twirling and spinning with each step. "There are monsters here, too. They're going to find a way to stop us."

"How do you know that, Gracie?" I ask. It's impossible to smother the concern in my voice, but she doesn't miss a beat.

"The voices told me."

That's when I make eye contact with Ansel and realise we're both thinking the same thing: the Forest is affecting more than just Gracie's body. If she's already speaking to voices in her head, who knows how her mind will deteriorate over the next few days.

Ansel's eyes fix helplessly on me. He doesn't have a story that can fix this situation and make it nothing more than a fairytale.

I clear my throat. Gracie's gaze shifts in my direction, but her eyes don't quite reach mine. "Well, don't let the voices drive you insane."

"Only some of them can drive," she says absent-mindedly. "Most of them are underage."

With that, we set off into the trees. I can't help but notice that the sun doesn't fully set.

TWO

As we continue our journey, the temperature begins to drop. The air leaves an icelike lace on our skin, moisture in the air freezing the second it makes contact. One half of the sky is washed with watery grey light illuminated by the partially sunk sun. The other half is a matte black canvas with no stars. Other than us and the darkness, all that exists is the harsh bite of the wind that can't be blocked out by our clothes.

We build a campfire, but the heat is sucked into the frigid air before it can reach our frozen hands. We add more wood and poke it with sticks and watch it die

21

a little each time. The light cast by the flames dances across the tree trunks, twisting and curling in obscure shapes. The fire itself is pulsating, matching every dip and sweep, the glowing embers moving in rhythm with the flames. It's mesmerising to watch: an array of orange and red giving way to burning white near the centre, like the fire is charming our worries from us and sending them away with the dark smoke.

Ansel lies on a fallen tree with his arms folded across his chest, rocking side to side and whimpering. He no longer needs to sleep, but that doesn't stop nightmares from plaguing his waking hours. His eyes are screwed shut with determination to escape from this world, even if it's just for a few minutes. I wonder what he's thinking about as he lies there, if he thinks about his family, his home, or if his thoughts have become consumed by what's going to happen to us.

Gracie sits by his feet, kicking the air, legs clearing the ground by several inches as they swing back and forth. Her face has an unhealthy greying look to it, and her hazel eyes are hard as she stares at nothing in the distance.

"Are you alright, Gracie?" I ask, reaching out to rest my hand on her shoulder. She stills for a moment.

"No." The word spills out of her lips like an accident. Her eyes lose their harshness, becoming rounder, glossier. Then her face crumbles all at once, the rise and fall of her chest stopping momentarily as the tears begin to stream. She hits my hand away from her, stands up, and runs off into the trees. Ansel opens his eyes briefly at the sound of commotion but decides not to go after her.

He told me earlier that Gracie knows something about the Forest, something big that she doesn't want to tell anyone. He said that giving her space would eventually make her want to tell her secrets. I don't think so, but there's nothing else for us to do.

The other boy is sitting beside me on a log, alert like a guard dog, close enough for us to be sitting together but still keeping his distance. The hairs on his arms are raised, and the bite of the wind has left goosebumps across his skin. I imagine that the bite is more than flesh-deep: blood running cold through his veins and his bones becoming chilled. The flames of the fire may look like they're burning warm, but the heat refuses to reach our skin.

"Do you want to rest for a bit?" I ask, wondering if the chill is also working its way inside of me, although I managed to carry a well-loved sweatshirt into the afterlife. It was the sweatshirt that I had died in.

The boy shakes his head frantically, unruly hair falling into his eyes. They're hard to see against the darkness of his skin but purple welts are scattered across his arms like a disease, a new one for each day we've been awake in the Forest. A bruise that began as a purple stain above his eyebrow has sunk into the socket and now appears to be a black eye. He's stopped rubbing at them, so I hope he's not in pain.

"Why not?"

Then, the boy opens his mouth and whispers the first words he's said since we arrived in the Forest. "I don't want to close my eyes." He accompanies this with a dry laugh, almost as if he's mocking himself. His voice is rusty—husky—from misuse. "My mind has the scary capability of being dark and demented."

"You're afraid of your dreams?"

"Yes," he whispers. His eyes fill with shadows as if he's seeing the darkness right now. I resist the urge to look behind me. "Who isn't?"

With that, the conversation is over. I stand and brush dead leaves off my jeans, wincing as a crisp edge scrapes my hand. Ansel offers to find Gracie.

We keep moving.

Gracie was right: we aren't alone in the Forest.

The first monsters appear as we reach our third rest stop. By now, the Forest has changed again, sprouting leaves the colours of flames and grass adorned with splashes of white flowers. An unnatural choking mist swirls and sprawls across the Forest floor, trapping protruding tree roots within its grasp. The bark now has the appearance of driftwood, twisting in patterns that remind me of ocean waves. Even the moss is kelp-like. It's soft and damp, yet my fingers come away dry.

The dying embers of sunlight streak through the leaves in shadowy beams, but the fog casts it into the sepia tones of aged photographs.

The Forest could have become one of those beautiful photographs. That was until Ansel claimed he spotted something moving in the distance.

"Stop!" he demands suddenly, throwing out his arms to stop us from taking another step. "There's someone straight ahead. I think they're walking towards us."

I squint into the distance, wondering how Ansel could barely see without glasses a few days ago, but now he can see through a sheet of white. "Are you sure? I can't see anything."

"I'm sure. It doesn't really look like a person anymore, but it's definitely something."

That's when I see it: a figure moving towards us in the distance. As it approaches, the shapeless blur expands.

"Well, I'm wrong. It's actually three somethings."

The monsters advance upon us. We don't do much

to escape from them. With each slow movement, slime drips from their skin, oozing puddles of white onto the ground, turning delicate flowers into decaying mush. The sickly substance is like the maggot-like texture of the eyes of a dead man, ready to burst at the slightest touch after being forgotten in his apartment for a few months. Not like I've seen a dead person before, but my sister and I used to make up stories about what could've happened to the old man upstairs when no one had seen him for a while.

"Shouldn't we be running?" Ansel asks, his breathing dissolving from stable into erratic. Gracie shuffles away from him and towards me instead. The other boy's body has tensed as if he's preparing for a fight.

We should be, but fear freezes my feet into the ground. Sweat drenches my skin. I can't ignore the throbbing of my eyes, the ringing echoing in my ears, the thumping of my heart in my throat. Gracie's hand slips into mine, the bitten stumps of her nails digging into my palms as I curl it into a fist. I can't hear the words I murmur to comfort her over the sound of blood rushing through my head, but I feel the oxygen flowing in and out of my lungs. In and out. In and out. In and out.

"We can't run," I say eventually. "They will know the Forest a lot better than us and there must be more of them somewhere else. Running would just be delaying the inevitable."

"What are we going to do?" Ansel's eyes are glossy and I wonder if he's holding back tears or wondering if he should run and leave the rest of us to our fate.

"There's nothing we can do."

I may say that, but I instantly begin making a list of all the things we could do in this situation. None of them are appealing.

The monsters get closer, and I get a clearer look at their appearance: a foot-long beak between the eyes caused by the prolonged heads; a mouth that opens downwards, armed with terrific mandibles; pair of enormous compound eyes like enormous crystals of cut glass; a shapeless body resembling a six-foot-tall maggot with flaps of concave skin covering the stomach; a stench of sewage and rotting flesh, potent enough for the boy to take a few steps back and retch dryly at his feet.

That's when I notice a teenage girl standing a few steps behind me. Well, a teenage girl with transparent skin, standing in a pool of smoke. I wouldn't have noticed her if the Forest seen through her body wasn't a scarred skeleton of reality. The Forest is painted in an array of orange and brown, but the world seen through her is burnt, the ashes still smoking. The smoke pool makes no sound as she drifts across the Forest floor, only parting to swallow up her feet. Dead leaves whisper from under the skin of the mist.

A sudden gush of pain jolts through my body, and an acidic burn spreads across my skin. My stomach convulses, my vision swims with black dots, and my legs give out from under me. I drop to the ground and slam painfully against a protruding root. My tongue is soaked with my blood. Bruised and winded with a body now in agony, I grab the closest thing that will serve as a weapon—a fallen tree branch—and thrust it forward, feeling it connect with something soft. I shut my eyes and push harder until nothing is resisting the force. When I open my eyes again, there is nothing in front of me beside the branch with the end coated in thick white slime.

One down, two left. And the mysterious smoke girl whose body trembles in the breeze.

The boy has the same idea as me. In the empty second between standoff and fighting, I see his eyes flick from me to the monster. His face is unreadable: no fear, no invitational smirk. His expression doesn't change as he steps forwards and plunges his branch into the next monster's stomach. He shows no signs of remorse as the body caves in around the branch and breaks apart like putty.

We forget about the third monster until we hear Ansel's scream. I turn around and the monster's claws wrap around his forearm, the bare skin charring from beneath its touch. We stand frozen with fear, wondering what's going to happen to him as soon as the monster lets go.

After a few more seconds, the monster collapses to the ground, its body crumbling beneath it. Ansel drops to his knees, shouting hoarsely and clutching at his arm—the shape of the monster's skeletal handprint has burned into his flesh. Gracie runs to Ansel's side, stabbing at what remains of the monster's chest with a stick as she passes, reducing its form to a pile of grey ashes. Her knuckles are white from her tight grip as if she's afraid to let go.

I'm still afraid, but I loosen my grip around my branch, noticing that the bumps on the surface have imprinted themselves into my palm. It was a good weapon in the moment. Hopefully, I won't need one again for a while.

When I turn around to hurl the branch away, the smoke girl is still standing a short distance behind us. Her eyes meet mine for a moment before her body dissolves and evaporates into the mist. I blink, and then she's gone.

THREE

"Sometimes, I think I remember what it was like. You know, *before*."

As the four of us advance further into the Forest, the trees close in around us. Here, the light has almost vanished completely: only fragments of illuminated sky remain, visible through the ragged canopy of trees above. A few stars wink through the blackness, and the moon is a waxed white crescent. The air is heavy with the perfume of the trees, a sharp freshness with an undertone of rot, and the scent of a dozen unfamiliar flowers unfurling their petals in the dark. Part of the ground has dissolved into a brook, and the sound of running water has the same hypnotic quality as the ocean. We pause to drink in the sound.

The grass is thigh high and cluttered with giant thistles and oversized ferns. I kick through the undergrowth until I'm at the edge of the brook, and then I take off my shoes and tuck my socks into my pockets, dipping my toes into the water. Gracie does the same, wobbling on one foot as she tugs at her shoe straps. Ansel grabs her arm to steady her and adds to his first thought. "While we're walking, I daydream about how I got here."

Gracie doesn't process his words and splashes downstream through the brook. Ansel, the boy, and I step aside so we can talk in some privacy. Gracie seems to know a lot about the Forest, but she doesn't know much—or anything—about us. We agreed to spare her from the harsh details of our real lives until this life becomes harsher.

"I remember how I got here," I say. The memory of that fatal afternoon comes back in flashes: the bottles, the pills, the needles. There was blood too, far more than what I imagined could fit inside my body. It wasn't just the drugs that killed me. "I have a lot of masochistic tendencies that make me feel like I'm truly alive rather than just floating through life."

I go into detail about the last real day of my life, from what I said to my mother when she left for work to the exact microwave meal I used to cover up the taste of her secret stash of cigarettes. Then the first few sleeping pills. Then the bite of the heroin. I tell them all that I can remember until the memory goes hazy, and I conclude that that's the moment when my heart stopped beating.

Ansel tells Gracie's story before his own, recounting the childlike, simplified version of events. She remembers everything from the moment the driver of the car—her brother—swerved into oncoming traffic to him crying beside her hospital bed, trying to nestle a teddy bear into her broken arms.

When Ansel tells his story, he doesn't share any details. "I've tried to take my own life a few times before, but this is the first time I've come close to actually dying."

"How'd you do it?" He seems too young to have experimented with substance abuse like me, but I'm still curious.

He rolls his eyes. "Sorry, but you have to be a level five friend or higher to unlock my full backstory."

The joke falls flat, and I see a hint of a scared boy beneath, desperate to be liked, desperate to be alive. I turn away from him and towards the other boy, hoping to remove the lingering awkwardness in the air. "How did you end up here?"

The boy slumps motionless against a tree, one hand caught in the brook's current, his mane of hair shielding his bruised eyes. His skin is tinged with grey, and it's difficult to believe that he's not already dead. Could this be what his body looks like in the real world? But then I hear the rattle of his breathing. He drags his gaze upwards and opens his mouth to speak, but Ansel cuts him off before he can say anything.

"Sorry for interrupting, but who are you? What's your name? How old are you?"

"August." The boy's unnaturally blue eyes glint like metal in sunlight. "Not after the month, but after the first Roman emperor."

I didn't notice before—how could I—but this voice is low and has more strength than his frail body suggests. He makes words sound like every syllable is a story.

"I'm seventeen, not born in August. I have a brain tumour the size of a golf ball, and it could be the last day of my life soon, but that's not why I'm here. I guess you'll have to wait and find out."

August winks at Ansel, and Ansel's face burns red. He quickly turns to find Gracie, demanding that we must keep moving. August chuckles to himself before returning to his previous silence, casting me a small smile as he looks away.

This boy is growing on me.

A few hours later, we stand at the edge of a ravine, an overwhelming sense of vertigo flooding through my veins. The ground ripples beneath me like waves.

If the Forest is playing a game with us, it has found my weakness: I am afraid of heights. Standing at the brink of the ravine reminds me of what implanted this fear deep into my mind.

In my memory, I am seven years old, standing in front of the bathroom mirror with a pair of nail clippers, attempting to trim my hair. I always wore it a little long so the dandelion fluff curls would straighten, but it had grown to the point where I had to keep flicking it out of my eyes.

From the bathroom, I could hear my younger siblings in the main room. Clara and Rose, four-year-old twins, played with the series of cardboard boxes taped together that served as their dollhouse and Jacob, only a few months old in this memory, gurgled in his bassinet. My older sister, Rowan, was hanging out laundry to dry on the rooftop patio.

Our house wasn't big. To be honest, it was just an

apartment. We had a large main room, a bathroom, and two small bedrooms—one for the girls and one for the boys. The battered sofa pulled out into a bed where our mother and her new husband slept when they weren't working. Most nights, they were, so my siblings and I pulled our bedding into the main room to build blanket forts and have 'sleepovers' together on the carpet.

Every apartment in the building was sparsely furnished and full of 'problem' families. They often consisted of young parents who struggled with addictions, adults who raised their grandchildren as their own when the parents were unable, and single mothers with more children than they could afford to deal with. We were the last family: it was a few years later when I became part of the problem.

As I stood in front of the mirror, I wondered what people meant when they said I looked like my father. I had never met him, and neither had the twins. There were three different fathers for three different pregnancies who cleared off the moment they found out my mother was expecting. She married Jacob's father shortly before his birth and that man, Michael, was the one who became our father. He was the one who stayed. He loved all of us like we were his flesh and blood.

I wanted to talk to my older sister about this, the men who came in and out of our lives. Was it true when the woman upstairs muttered about Michael only being a temporary member of our family? Was it true when the girls at school said he'd leave like the rest of our fathers? Was it true when the man in the hallway grabbed me by the collar and hissed that my mother trapped Michael with a pregnancy to take his money? People couldn't accept that this man could genuinely care for us while expecting nothing in return.

I finished trimming my hair with an uneven snip above my eyebrows and walked out into the stairwell, half-closing the door to the apartment behind me. The door locked the moment it was fully closed, and neither of the twins were tall enough to reach the handle and open it again from the inside. We also lost the spare key a few days after we moved in.

I set off up the stairs, taking the first couple of flights two steps at a time before I became breathless enough to pull myself up the last few using the broken bannister. I kept climbing until I reached the roof, the place where everyone gathered to do laundry in the summer, hanging it out on washing lines to air dry.

My mother insisted that there was a resemblance between me and Rowan, but I never saw one. She was a fairytale princess in my childlike eyes, with thick dark curls that she inherited from her father, large brown eyes, and golden beige skin, the opposite of me and our mother and the rest of our siblings. She also had a kindness that couldn't be genetic, patience with me that was learned and not inherited. She was the best of us.

"Hey, Oli," she said when she saw me, most likely relieved that I was there to help her with the chores. I didn't realise how you could see her ribs through her thin dress when she lifted her arms to hang holey socks on the line. She shrunk her portion sizes at dinner to make sure everyone else had more.

"Hi," I replied, forgetting what I had wanted to ask. My attention was drawn to a filthy rag doll on the other side of Rowan, abandoned on the rusting railing that ran along the edges of the roof. It was the kind of handmade doll that both of the twins wanted to own, or wanted Rowan to teach them how to sew one day, even if it looked as if it would break apart as soon as something touched it.

I could see the doll slipping across the railing in the breeze until I was sure it was going to fall. Darting across the roof before my mind could catch up, I threw myself at the doll and grabbed it. I miscalculated my leap and launched myself straight at the fragile railing.

"Oliver!"

I felt Rowan's hand seize a fistful of my t-shirt and drag me backwards as the effort shoved her forward.

She didn't scream as her body hit the ground and broke in an unfixable way.

I wrap my arm around a tree to keep my balance as I inhale deeply, closing my eyes and trying to push the memory into nonexistence. We must keep moving, and choking down my fear is the only way to do that.

"Are you okay?" Gracie whispers to me as Ansel plots our route into the ravine. She tugs on my sleeve until I bend down to her level. Her eyes are wide with concern.

I force myself to smile. It's unconvincing, but it's good enough for her. "I'm fine. Let's get going."

So we go.

We're a third of the way into the ravine when I contemplate what we're doing. I'm not thinking about why we're climbing into a massive tear into the ground instead of finding a way around it. I'm thinking about why we're bothering to go down when the world could change at any moment and trap us beneath the surface forever.

We're two-thirds of the way into the ravine when my vertigo returns in full force, my vision swimming with each step. The fear of being so high up is my motivation to keep going down towards the bottom—towards safety—and it's a lot quicker to climb into a ravine and out the other side than trail around the edge until we find an alternative route. It's my motivation not to slip and fall like Rowan which keeps me taking tentative steps forward, gripping onto Gracie's hood for comfort.

The final third takes the longest. We stop to observe our progress and any changes in the environment regularly. Jagged ledges of rock stick out from the ravine wall and I think I see a stream of water at the base of the other wall, glowing a fluorescent cyan blue. I can make out the shapes of bright emerald grass and trees that almost look like regular beech trees, just with an array of comic book-bright leaves in all shades of the rainbow: orange and yellow and green and pink, sometimes purple or blue. The colours shift as the leaves flutter in the breeze.

We're at the bottom of the ravine when Ansel drops into the long grass at the bottom, takes a few steps, and then stops.

"There's someone else down here."

The person on the ground is lifeless, and it's Gracie who realises that.

Lifeless.

The body is slumped over, half sitting, half lying in a patch of weeds at the base of a tree. The auburn hair is missing in large patches, stained crimson with dried blood. Without eyelids, the milky brown irises stare into the sky while the lipless mouth hangs open. The corpse itself is almost devoid of skin, and the ribcage is caving in from burrowing insects and where a tree root has grown through the bones. I turn away as my stomach heaves, nostrils filled with the smell of decaying meat. My heart pounds as one question races through my mind, but Gracie is the one to ask it.

"Who did this?"

She crouches down and presses her hands against what remains of the chest as if she can convince the heart to beat again. An insect crawls across her hand and leaves flakes of blood in its path, but she barely flinches, only screws her eyes shut in determination.

No one tries to stop her. She stays like that for a while. Ansel quickly grows bored and lies in the grass, staring at the dark sky with empty eyes. August disappears to examine the rest of the ravine.

I remain by Gracie's side, watching her every move, trying to figure out her every thought. I still wonder why she seems to know so much about the Forest. I wonder how she knows things and how much of what she knows could be the truth.

For a moment, I think I see something. A spark, maybe. It could just be wishful thinking, but I think I see patches of the skin beginning to stitch back together beneath Gracie's hands, the chest starting to rise and fall with breath...

The spark flickers out as fast as it appeared.

Gracie collapses into the grass, hands stained with patches of dried blood, brow furrowed in confusion. Whatever she was trying to do, she thought it would work. She *knew* it could work.

I don't have the chance to ask her anything because August appears from between the trees, his hair even more unruly and littered with leaves, his face flushed as if he's been running. "You should all come with me. I think I've found something."

FOUR

We follow August inside a tunnel that slices cleanly through the rock. Inside, it is pitch black and I walk with my hand resting on his shoulder, trusting him to lead the way. Gracie's fingers are clutching at my belt loop, and Ansel is somewhere behind her, grabbing onto her coat hood. Loose stones litter the ground and we send them scattering with each step, the sound peppering off the walls like gunshots. As we descend into the tunnel, the absence of light means the absence of warmth, so I concentrate on the heat of August's skin through his t-shirt. He barely flinches when my grasp tightens.

After minutes of walking, the tunnel doesn't change. I cope with the darkness for a while, ignoring how it presses down on me, humming songs I no longer remember the words to as a distraction. It's as if I'm standing in a room, and the ceiling and all four walls are inching closer and closer with no way to escape. I'm not afraid of the dark or confined spaces, but I have a fear of things that lurk where they can't be seen.

Now, that fear is irrational since I'm trapped in a world of perpetual half-light, full of decomposing corpses and monsters that burn their mark into your skin.

My mother always taught me to fear the dark. She forgot to mention the horrors that live in the light.

Seconds drag into minutes. Minutes melt into what feels like hours. The tunnel twists to the left before suddenly veering back to the right, and I can no longer tell if we're approaching the surface or heading deeper into the ground. All I know is that there is now something glowing in the distance, a light that is only a flash of gold on a canvas of black. It looks like candlelight.

"We're almost there," August mutters, mostly to himself, as I'm about to point out my observation. I'm not sure where *there* is, but at least it's not in this tunnel.

We soon enter a small cavern illuminated by the warm golden glow of three candles spread out evenly around the space. Someone must've been here recently. The walls arch fifty feet up to giant stalactites and bat roosts. There's a table against the far wall and an image crudely drawn in charcoal on fraying cloth lays in the centre.

In the middle of the cloth, there is a large circle, a line splitting it in half and another line splitting one half into quarters. Small shapes and symbols decorate the blank spaces between the lines. On the semicircle side, someone has scrawled a circle in the centre with a square above and below it. A messy triangle is beside the line which splits the semicircle in half. The shapes must have a code, but the maker of what I assume to be a map didn't leave a note to say what they represent.

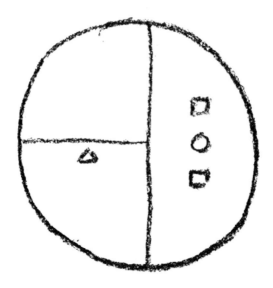

"This has to be the Forest," August ponders, tracing his finger around the edge of the biggest circle. He then moves on to the smaller shapes. "These have to be important places like camps or other caves like this. They could be places where people are, couldn't they?"

Gracie is too short to have a clear view of the map, so she rests her chin on the edge of the table and squints while August tilts it up for her. "What do the lines mean?"

"I'm not sure. They could be boundaries or a way of showing different areas of the Forest. If I'm right and the shapes mark important places, we could be here." His finger drifts towards the triangle and then hovers above the shorter line. "This could be the ravine."

Gracie looks at him as if he holds all the answers to this strange world. My expression shifts to match hers. Ansel looks less than impressed. "Why aren't any of you looking at the book?"

Three pairs of eyes flick towards him. He rubs at the handprint burnt into his arm as he stares at a spot on the ground. I look, and there's a trunk hidden behind the table, a leather-bound book—more like a journal—resting on top. The trunk itself is coated in an inch thick of dust, but the book looks clean as if someone handled it recently.

"Why don't *you* look at the book? We're looking at the map." August rolls his eyes and returns to the map, describing his theories to Gracie. His tone grows more confident as her smile widens and her timid nods become more enthusiastic.

Ansel sighs and walks to the other side of the cavern, presumably to sulk, so I'm the one who looks at the book.

Bound in faded red leather, cracked and dry with age, the thin book smells faintly of tobacco and rose perfume. The pages are brittle, and what remains of the book's original stitching is barely holding it together. A faded scrawl on the inside cover declares who the journal once belonged to, but the name has become lost to time. The first page begins in the middle of a sentence, and the book's poor condition makes it impossible to tell if there are missing pages or if another book existed before this one.

Handmade paper rustles as I thumb through the pages, looking for nothing in particular. Words appear and disappear as my eyes flit across the pages, trying to pick out anything of importance from the jumble of sentences. When nothing stands out, I snap the book shut and tuck it into my waistband for safekeeping. I join Ansel near the cavern entrance.

He's staring into the emptiness, squinting as if he needs his glasses again. He's standing so still that it looks like he might've stopped breathing.

"Are you okay, Ansel?" I ask.

He doesn't respond for a moment, but then he shakes his head as if he's snapping himself out of a daydream. "I thought I saw something, that's all."

When I look into the tunnel, I see that the darkness isn't as empty as I thought. It's full of movement: dark grey *things* detaching themselves from the black before reuniting with the shadows. I step back and try to hide better as I count the shapes. Ten? Twenty? Maybe more?

"What are they?" I murmur to no one, hearing August and Gracie stop talking behind me. August joins me, standing right in the middle of the entrance. I try to pull him back, the same way I would if one of my siblings was in danger, but he shakes himself free of my grasp. I must remember that he is nothing like my family, my friends, even if there's something inside that pushes me towards him.

"Monsters," he states, quickly counting the shapes before darting to the back of the cavern. He pulls out the trunk from beneath the table and I see that there are weapons hidden beneath layers of cloth. Knives.

Swords. Even a bow with a half-full quiver of arrows.

"What do we do?" I glance briefly up the tunnel and then follow August in his hunt for weapons. Ansel has already spread a selection of blades across the floor. Gracie peers over his shoulder with a tentative gaze.

"We're going to fight them, aren't we?" August says to me.

"What? How are you expecting us to do that?"

He rolls his eyes. "We have weapons this time. Grab something sharp. Aim. Fire. These monsters look different from the other ones, more human."

"And how does that help me?"

He hesitates, then thrusts a sword into my hands. "It's easier to break something when you can use your weaknesses against it."

The monsters are further away than we expected. After walking through the tunnel, I remember how I thought the flickering candlelight was close even though it was just an illusion, so far out of our reach.

Holding my borrowed sword in one hand, I swing it uncertainly a few times. It feels very different to sword fighting in the kitchen with mops and brooms against Rowan. The twins were always our spectators, dressing us for battle in armour made of tinfoil, our biggest fans in the imaginary world we created. I shake myself free of the memory and press my back against the wall beside the entrance.

I wait.

August stands on the opposite side, shooting glances up the tunnel. His sword is drawn, and I copy his fighting stance. The weapon looks natural in his hands.

We wait.

From my position, I can hear the monsters move in perfect synchronisation, fascinating and terrifying. They could be machines being controlled by one giant mind. August seems to think this too. His eyes widen, and he runs across to my side of the entrance.

"They're not monsters," he gasps into my ear, making sure no one else can hear. "They're human, aren't they?"

"What do you mean?"

57

He swallows sharply, and I risk looking into the tunnel. He's right: they look more like people than the monsters we encountered in the trees. They're dressed in black and stained with dirt. Weapons are slung across their shoulders, tucked into pockets, and clutched in gloved hands.

"August. What do you mean?"

"Isn't it obvious? They're teenagers. And they don't look happy to see us."

Soon, they're only thirty feet away from us. I hide behind an overturned table with Gracie huddled protectively by my side. August and Ansel stand on either side of the entrance with their backs against the wall, one with a sword in hand and the other with a bow and a knife.

We watch in silence as the teenagers enter the cavern and fan out in a rough semicircle, a few standing behind to block the only exit. There could be more of them further up the tunnel waiting for us if we escape. Running is no longer an option. We must fight, even though we're inexperienced and outnumbered.

All their expressions are identical. Their faces are emotionless, resembling the stone wall behind them. Their reptilian eyes are empty.

A girl steps forward and speaks in a voice as monotone as her expression. "We are sent here in order to collect you on the behalf of our leader," she states. She doesn't look any older than thirteen. "The reason is unknown."

I duck down further behind the table and pull Gracie closer to my side, even though they must know that this is the only place for us to hide. It's too late to run. My grip tightens on the hilt of my sword.

"You have been given the choice to come willingly or forcefully."

August's eyes glint at me in the candlelight. He nods slowly. I hope I understand what he means.

Forcing myself to stand, I look directly into the girl's empty eyes. "I guess you're going to have to take us forcefully."

Before I can say anything else, Ansel sinks an arrow into the base of her skull. She falls like a marionette with the strings cut. Her body hits the floor. She doesn't get back up. Ansel winces as he fires another arrow, but I can't tell if it's from the fear of missing his target or the fear of hitting it again.

August explodes, throwing himself towards the nearest person, his sword slicing viciously through the air. He aims straight for their throats. That should be deadly enough, but they're more prepared and their weapons have longer blades with more cutting area than ours do. One carries a double-headed axe. One hit, not even a good one, and the fight will be over.

I will myself to do something, even if it's just to protect Gracie. These people may appear to be human, but that doesn't stop them from being monsters.

I raise my sword and hear an empty thud as it hits a girl who looks alarmingly like my younger sisters. She looks down to where the blade presses against her chest and smiles. I didn't hit flesh. She's not wearing armour; her body is made of metal. Shocked by the unexpected barrier, I'm off-balance and try to pivot. A mechanical leg swipes out, and I trip, the ground rushing towards me. There is nothing to cushion my fall.

The impact is agonising. I lose my grip on my sword, and then I'm lying on my back and gasping for breath with it landing beside my head. My left hand is on fire, my wrist screeching with burning pain, and my fingers are completely numb. I gasp in a frantic breath. I try to push myself up with one hand, but my arm buckles beneath my weight, and I fall back down on the injured wrist. Broken? Fractured? Maybe it's just the nerves…

But where is the girl? Where is Gracie? My head swirls in panic, and I ignore the pain that sears through my bones. Both feel as if they are going to kill me.

Gracie is a few feet away. She is uninjured besides a single trail of blood dripping down her forearm, her raincoat sleeve torn to reveal her brown skin. Three of the mechanical teenagers are laying at her feet. I don't give myself time to think about how she did that, because I sense the girl who knocked me down. Before I can process what's happening, I roll over just in time to avoid a blade whipping past my face. It collides with the ground beneath me. The force sends sparks up her arms. I kick out my leg and hook it around hers, tugging her down. She gasps as she falls onto me. Desperately, I try to catch a blow on her body, but I keep encountering metal plates protecting her. There is nothing left that I can do to save myself.

Unless…

I position my sword in front of my face, using the blade to block attacks from the girl, now straddling my waist. She slashes wildly with her weapon as if she's following a pattern. Her metallic joints creak with the movement and I wonder how much of her is human and how much is a machine. I wonder if she's lost all her humanity or if she still has the desire for human needs, like warmth and thirst and sleep.

If she does, she doesn't for much longer. An arrow fired from the far side of the cave pierces the strip of soft skin on the back of her neck. She falls to the side and August appears from nowhere to slice his blade cleanly through her throat. Her body convulses once, then it falls still.

I roll away from her body and lift my head, not wanting to hurt my arm any more than it already is. August stands at my side, hair forming a halo of curls around his face and his eyes illuminated with triumph. He looks relieved to see that I'm still alive.

"Are you hurt?"

I point to my side. "Arm."

He drops to his knees and furrows his brow as he examines my arm, cradling my wrist in his hands, moving up to my elbow when he sees nothing wrong. "It doesn't look broken. Maybe the Forest has magical healing properties."

Suddenly, he leans forward and collapses against my chest, wrapping his arms around my waist, pressing the hidden book uncomfortably into my stomach. Despite the lingering pain in my arm, I try to hug him back, my heart fluttering at the first physical affection I've felt in days. His touch somehow makes the cave warmer, and I feel more hopeful about our survival.

"Those people were not people, they were machines," I whisper into his ear. "Someone sent them after us, and

63

we should be dead now, but they were barely fighting back. It's like they were testing us."

August nods against my chest, and his hair tickles my chin. He looks up slightly and his cheeks are damp with tears, eyes reddening and eyelashes spiky. It reminds me that we're all just kids.

"I read a book about something like them once. Someone kidnapped people during the Industrial Revolution and transformed them into mechanical soldiers. They were supposed to be immortal workers because they had no heart." He slips from my embrace and rubs at his face with the back of his hand, casting a glance up the tunnel. I look too, but all I can see is darkness. "We can't stay here for much longer—whoever sent them will send more."

With that, we stand and pick up our weapons, grabbing the map from the table before we head back into the tunnel.

FIVE
AUGUST

I walk with the map held in both hands, trying to decipher the markings to stop my mind from wandering towards child soldiers and human machines and wrapping my arms around Oliver. If my focus slips, I feel the ghost of the memory of my hair brushing Oliver's cheeks and his heartbeat beneath my head. Slow and steady.

The trees ripple with iridescence, and the half-light shining through the leaves casts colours across my skin like the stained-glass windows in the church from the bright summers of my childhood. But the colours aren't real. Nowadays, I'm not sure if my memories are.

The problem with hallucinations is their unpredictability. I'd stand more of a chance of figuring out my reality if they were always the same thing showing up at the same time of day, or if they were very clear that the things clouding my vision were not real. My mind, however, has become far more creative since waking up in the Forest: the hallucinations show up at any time and manifest as anything.

They are always colours, the patches of technicolour across my skin that started the whole thing before I even knew that there was something wrong inside of me. They are either a warning signal of what is coming or the cause. I wait for the next 'thing' to come. If the colours are vibrant, the hallucination will be friendly, even funny. If they are dull, then everything after that will be a horror show that I can't pause.

They are also getting progressively less amusing. Now, I see an apparition, barely a distortion of a light beam, a human cut out of colours that aren't quite right. When it moves, the trees behind it look burned, as if the world has been set alight. As quickly as it appears, it vanishes without leaving so much as a phantom footprint in the undergrowth. It feels unholy, so I cross myself, shrug away the memory, and then keep walking.

But it's back again in a second, lingering this time, so I can get a clear look at it. It looks like a teenage girl hovering a few inches above the ground, unless her feet are just swallowed in the pool of smoke beneath her. Something tells me that she might be more than a hallucination.

I keep walking with the map held in both hands, pretending to decipher a series of squares so no one else notices that I fix my attention on the girl. The trees ripple with charcoal and smoke through her skin, and the half-light shining through the leaves casts fake colours across my arms. Fake colours, but a potentially real girl. A girl who is gesturing for me to follow her into the trees.

I want to stick to the path; I know the rules for walking through the Forest and leading the group astray isn't one of them. However, the desire to find out if she's real is almost uncontrollable, the hope that something might finally not be part of my imagination or my illness.

Casting one more look towards the smoke girl, I tilt the map towards my chest, hiding the markings from view, and follow her path instead.

SIX

"We're lost."

"Ansel, we're in some kind of magical Forest that changes every day with no known way of escaping. We didn't know where we were in the first place."

"But *he*," he glares at August, "found the map and decided he knew what it meant. We followed him, and now we're lost."

I inhale sharply. "We're not lost. We're going in the direction we decided, but we don't know the exact scale of the map. We could almost be there—wherever *there* is—or it could be forever away. Are you going to keep

73

walking, or should we leave you alone to complain to the monsters?"

Ansel, August, and I stop walking. Gracie trots along ahead, oblivious to the argument that is taking place.

"I am going to walk for ten more minutes in this direction. Alone. Well, with Gracie. If there's nothing there…" He drifts off before he can think of a worse threat than being lost in some kind of magical Forest that changes every day with no known way of escaping. Then he must decide that a threat isn't worth his time because he turns on his heel and disappears into the trees after Gracie.

August and I stay put. The brook is yet to fade from existence, so we make the most of our rest stop, taking off our shoes and wrapping the book in my sweatshirt for safety and sitting on the grass so we can dip our toes into the water. The sudden coolness is relaxing.

I look up at the trees that stretch out their limbs over the brook until they touch fingers. Moss hangs in swathes of green-grey from the branches. I reach up to touch a low-hanging piece, and it's softer than my favourite jumper. A dozen orange moths chase fireflies into the sunset side of the sky. Something about this strange world reminds me of home.

"Can I trade you a bad memory for a good one?" August asks after a few moments of comfortable silence. "I've got a lot on my mind right now."

I nod. "Say whatever you want. We have all the time in the world."

He breathes in deeply as if he's trying to calm his breathing. He closes his eyes.

"My family isn't broken in the typical sense, but that doesn't mean we don't need fixing," he begins, hands drifting to the bruises on his wrists. "I can tell you right now that we're far from perfect, and that was okay for a while until I was thirteen. Some kids at school beat me up for kissing another boy on the cheek after church." He rubs at the bruises on his arms as if they're reminders from that day. "My stepmother kept me home from school for a while, not for my safety, but to stop me from embarrassing her in public again.

"She sent me to the closest thing she could find to conversion therapy for a few months, and those were the darkest days of my life. For the first few weeks of being there, I learned to hate myself so that I was willing to change anything about myself just to be left alone. The therapists said that almost half their patients didn't live long enough to complete the process, and I found out that was true."

He pauses as his eyes fill with tears, but they're not from sadness: they're from anger. His voice shakes, and he grabs at both his elbows as if he's holding himself together before continuing. I wonder if the memory makes him feel weak.

"Every time we had a group session, I wondered who would be there and who would be dead because that's normal, isn't it? I met a nine-year-old there who vanished during my second week. He was the first person I ever knew who died. After him, they all blended together.

"The second stage of therapy is where they 'rebuild

your image', technically teaching you how to be anything other than what you were, than what you *are*. Anything other than gay. This stage never lasted long, because we were all so desperate to go home and it was easier to repress who we really were at that point. They taught us how to talk, dress, and act. They even taught us how to *eat*. They made us into shells of people, and I only got out of there because I was so good at pretending that they told my parents I was excited to be 'cured'. I never knew why what I did was wrong."

August rubs at his eyes with his knuckles, then glares at the tears as if he's ashamed. "I think we're here because we're dead. Maybe I'll be able to see all my friends again." His face burns red at the confession. "Actually, I'm sorry. Forget I told you that."

I cut him off before he can say any more and try to smile in a way that I hope shows comfort rather than sympathy. "No. You've made the trade. Now you just need to be quiet and listen to my memory, or the trade isn't fair."

I dip a hand into the brook as I contemplate the

good memories I have, picking through my most treasured ones in exchange for his most terrible. When I think of one, I close my eyes and allow myself to become immersed.

"When I was younger, my family didn't have much, but we had each other and a communal garden, and that felt like more than enough for us. There was a pine tree there and, near the end of summer, it would be covered in butterflies. Hundreds of monarchs rested there. My older sister and I would paint our skin with sugar water and reach out, and they'd crawl onto our arms, barely moving as they breathed. I'd spin in the sunlight and watch their wings glow like tiny candles. I had my first kiss and my last kiss beneath that tree, one with butterflies on my skin, the other with leaves the same colours as their wings falling around me."

Then it's not just the butterflies I can feel on my arms. There's the ghost of a hand resting on my waist, another tilting my chin upwards. There's a warm chest pressed against mine. There's a delicate kiss like a butterfly on my lips. It's so real, as if I'm seven years old and playing in the garden, as if I'm fourteen years old and climbing over the locked gate to have someone's hands on my hips and their lips on mine for the first time.

Before I reach the story's ending, I open my eyes. The butterflies fade into the orange sky. But we've made the trade: one awful inescapable thing for that golden moment in time, that moment of soft honeycomb light and a warm summer day tapering to an eternal evening. August doesn't have to bear his past alone anymore. Instead, I'll hold it for him while he looks at the butterflies.

The scent of the Forest—like pine needles after rain—drifts past me and I realise that while I've been thinking about August, August has been looking at me. He looks exhausted, as if carrying the burden of his bad memories has finally become too much for him. The half-sunk sun burns a golden crown around his head.

"I believe you, by the way," I say, turning towards him. "About the map."

"Thanks." He doesn't sound bitter, only tired. At least one person believes in him.

"But," I continue. A single dark eyebrow raises. "I also believe that the government is controlled by aliens, so I wouldn't hold my opinions to a high standard."

August shuffles closer to me. He leans in until his head rests in the crook of my neck. We close our eyes. Both of our breaths are shaking. I think I want to kiss him, for him to join me under my pine tree.

"Thank you," he says again, his voice low, nothing more than a whisper.

"For what?" My voice wavers.

"For being you."

My cheeks flush pink while his burn red. "You're welcome. Thanks again for saving my life in the cave."

August smiles, then he lifts his head, leans in closer, and gently kisses me, his lips warm against mine. The world walls away. In my mind, it's one of those endless summer afternoons. The kiss is slow and soft, comforting in ways that words will never be. He hesitates for a second before pulling away, taking a few shaky shallow breaths. I do the same.

"I didn't think you were gay," he says quietly, almost to himself.

I shrug.

"What does that mean?" His voice is a whisper in the breeze.

"I don't know." I close my eyes. Familiar faces blur against the back of my eyelids, the girls and boys who've held important places in my life. I squeeze my eyes shut until the faces are replaced with colourful static. "I guess I've never thought much about who I am. It doesn't really come up in conversation."

He laughs. I laugh with him, even though I'm not sure why.

"Are *you* gay?" I ask, looking over at him, still laughing. In this moment, he's beautiful. A boy made of gold.

"Completely."

"So, do you do this all the time?"

"Do what all the time?"

"Kiss boys."

The laughter stops abruptly. He rolls his eyes. "No."

"Then how do you know?"

"I just do. How do you *not* know?"

I lace my fingers through his and his thumb brushes against the back of my hand, rubbing circles into my knuckles. "I try not to think."

"About being gay?"

"About anything." My sister. My drugs. Dying. Living.

"Why?"

"Because," I say with a sigh, "it hurts too much to think about things that you can't have or help. It's better not to think about it."

He stops rubbing his thumb across my skin. "Are you going to try to not think about me?"

"No."

Yes.

I change the subject.

"Was that—" I begin. The words stick in my throat, and I wonder if the question is inappropriate. "Was that your first proper kiss?"

He raises an eyebrow as if to taunt me and I want to kiss him again. "No, I've been practising on random strangers in here." He grins and I swear I feel my heart skip a beat. "Yes. You're my first real kiss."

The moment apart doesn't last for much longer.

Within seconds, his lips brush mine again. Not innocently, but passionately and demanding. I want to pull away again before I find myself a new addiction, but I can't. My hands tangle in his hair, and I pull him deeper into the kiss. His hands work their way around my body, feeling every inch of skin under my t-shirt. His fingers run down my spine, tugging me closer until there is no space between us and I can feel the beating of his heart against my chest.

"Oliver," he whispers, prolonging each syllable. I smile, my heart fluttering at his voice as I clasp my hands on either side of his face. Never has my name sounded so lovely, I think, as I lean in for another...

"Oliver? August? We think we've found something."

Ansel and Gracie burst through the trees, their faces streaked with dirt and hair a mess of tangles.

August and I leap apart as if someone's shot electricity through us.

"There's a camp a few minutes away from here," Ansel says without making eye contact. I know he must've seen the kiss. "We should get moving before the Forest changes again—I think people are living there."

With that, he and Gracie rush off again. August and I remain sitting with our feet in the water, leaning against each other to catch our breath. His eyes close for a moment. I tilt his face upward and press my lips against his temple. My heart beats so hard I'm afraid he'll hear it.

"Oh no," I say suddenly, resting my hand against my chest as if it has the power to pause my racing pulse.

August's eyes open, his head snapping towards me. "What is it? What happened? Who died?"

"I think I just felt an emotion."

"You have got to be kidding me."

He rolls his eyes and starts to walk away, damp feet collecting leaves, shoes in one hand, clasping onto my wrist with the other, dragging me along behind him. I jog a few steps until we're side by side and lace our fingers back together. He tightens his grip, and his thumb returns to rubbing circles against my knuckles.

It's too soon to tell, but I think I could love him.

SEVEN

nsel and Gracie lead us to a lake. There's an island in the middle, but it's impossible to tell what could be on it besides the dark outline of trees silhouetted against a distant campfire. I hope that there is something hidden within them.

Ansel has the same idea as me. "There has to be something there, *someone* there. Everything in the Forest is here for a reason. Why else would you put an island in the middle of a lake?"

We just need to get over to it.

There's a small boat bobbing against the shoreline, only big enough for two people. By the time I walk over to it, Ansel has clambered inside, helping Gracie climb in beside him. He forces an apologetic smile. "Gracie can't swim, and she won't be able to row the boat on her own."

So August and I have to swim. We take off our shoes, strip down to our underwear, and abandon our clothes at the bottom of the boat. I hide the book under my discarded jeans. Gracie wraps my sweatshirt around her shoulders for extra warmth. August pushes the boat out into the water and steps back as Ansel dips in the oars and starts rowing towards the island.

We watch the boat from the shore, hearing snippets of stories float across the surface of the lake. When their voices fade, I look at August and then nod towards the island. "I'll race you."

He arches an eyebrow and smirks. "Oh, you will?"

I squeeze his hand three times as a silent countdown and we run towards the water: August diving, me following with a graceful cannonball. The water is ice-cold, and I clench my jaw shut to stop myself from shouting and swallowing lungfuls of water. We surface at the same time, him a few feet ahead of me, and he laughs hysterically when he sees my expression.

We're halfway to the island when we both decide to give up the race. The distance is farther than I've ever swum before, and August would rather float on his back while I tread water beside him, trying not to think about what kinds of creatures could brush against my feet.

In the half-light, his face is bathed in an amber glow, the permanently setting sun painting his skin golden, softening the harshness of his face. His hair floats like seaweed in the water, spreading out like a blackened halo. He looks like an angel. A fallen one, though, with a body marked by bruises from the journey down from heaven, but still an angel.

A shiver runs through me. I want to pull him close, to feel him relax in my arms again, to see his grin that's wild and beautiful in the half-light. I shouldn't want to, not after the memory he shared with me, but I can barely think about anything else if he's by my side, not even my survival. This isn't just a crush. This is something else.

I can't believe I'm falling in love as my life is ending.

August's ears are below the water, and he can't hear anything I say clearly, but that gives me the courage to tell him anyway. "You're beautiful."

He doesn't react until a minute or two later when he decides to start moving again. The race has ended, and it's just the two of us swimming side by side, trying to keep warm and stay afloat until the shoreline is within sight.

"You said something to me just now, didn't you?" he asks, flicking strands of wet hair out of his eyes. The light reflecting off the water makes them sparkle like how the ocean reflects the sun. I almost seize up until I remember I must keep swimming or I'll drown. I don't want to die twice. "What was it?"

"I said that you're beautiful," I tell him again with significantly less confidence than the first time, turning my head towards the moon and hoping that the darkness will disguise my blush. It doesn't.

He beams. It's the first time I've seen him smile so widely. "Don't lie to me."

My blush deepens, so I splash him as a distraction from my cheeks. He returns to laughing hysterically, wiping the water from his eyes with wet hands and making the situation worse. He dips briefly below the surface when his laughter becomes too intense and comes back up spluttering, although the smile is still on his face.

"I would never lie to you," I say, a smile forming on my own face. His grin is contagious, untamed, lifting the darkness that has taken refuge in his eyes. "I never lie to anyone."

"I know," he says, although he doesn't. He trusts me. "Let's keep swimming. Ansel won't send a search party if we don't turn up, will he?"

"I'll race you."

We see the campfire before we see the camp.

The wood is far longer than what should have been used. It's taller than us and burns with the smokiness of a funeral pyre. Flames leap high, and their crackling can be heard before August and I emerge from the lake. A half-empty bucket of steaming water sits beside the blaze, not even large enough to annoy the inferno.

But we don't care.

The chill has returned to the air, so we stand as close to the fire as we dare with Ansel and Gracie to feel the radiating warmth, holding out numb hands for defrosting, tugging dry clothes over damp bodies. Sparks fly into the sub-zero air only to die mid-flight.

A dishevelled tent sits a few feet away from the fire. The ropes that should have been tight have plenty of give in them, and the bottom sheet should have been pulled out taut when it was pegged in. With black clouds gathering and plunging the world into darkness, I can't judge the efforts of whoever set up the tent, although I wonder how recently they left if their fire is still burning. It may be no more than a pile of fraying green canvas, but it's the shelter we're going to need as soon as the rain begins to fall.

I look inside. There are two sleeping bags laid out on the ground, an empty wicker picnic hamper where Gracie has stored the book, and an ancient gas lamp that doesn't seem to work. The sleeping bags are threadbare and could be filled with bugs, but I lie down on one anyway, grateful for the slight comfort that feels like home.

August slips into the tent behind me, lying down on the other sleeping bag. He stares blankly at the tent roof for a few minutes before rolling over to face me. His eyes flicker in the campfire's light. I hadn't been paying attention to see them clearly before, but they're electric blue—not the kind of electric shock that paralyses you or crawls under your muscles, but the kind that makes your blood dance.

He allows me to stare into his eyes for a few moments longer before breaking the silence. "How's your arm?" He smiles again, but I can't tell why.

"It's better." I stretch out my arm and bend each joint a few times, only feeling the dull muscle ache from our swim.

"Good."

"Why?"

"So you can hold me again."

I laugh and he shuffles over to curl up in my arms, kicking the tent flap closed so we're shut off from the Forest. In the darkness, his presence is a glimpse of safety amongst the shadows. I wish I could pretend that Ansel and Gracie aren't going to come inside at any moment, so I can hold August for a while longer with his head pressed against my chest. It's the light in the darkness, a lone star in an otherwise empty sky. I don't think that I've ever felt this way before.

"Do you think we're moving too fast?" August asks as if he can read my thoughts. He tilts his head up to rest his chin on my shoulder. The blue of his irises is darkened by his eyelashes.

"What do you mean?"

"Well, we hugged for the first time, then kissed an hour or so later. We're cuddling now. Look, I'm gay, but I don't even know what your sexuality is."

I think about it and realise that I don't know either. I've always liked boys and girls just the same. "That doesn't matter. What do you think is more important right now: having a sexuality crisis or being trapped in a magical Forest with no way to escape?"

He takes a moment to think about this. "But I don't know how to be in love with someone. Or how to be loved by them. And I don't think you'd want that from me. I don't think you'd want *me*."

"That's fine," I say. "I understand."

"And I know you think we're doomed."

"Right now, we are."

"And I don't think you're gay." He taps his fingers across his lips as he considers this. "I mean, maybe you are, at least partly."

"No one cares if I'm gay," I say simply and then instantly regret my choice of words.

August sits up, and I watch his profile. His eyes narrow, and his mouth becomes a straight line.

"What I'm saying is…" My voice falters. "I like to look at you. I like *you*."

I lean closer to him. He turns towards me, taking my face in his hands. Kissing me. Grabbing me and not letting go.

For a moment, I think about someone else, then I remember that I'm a dimension away from them. And then I remember that I'm dead, so it doesn't matter if I'm betraying the complicated, barely-friends-or-almost-lovers aspect of our relationship. And then I think about whether this, what's happening right now, means that I'm gay. Or bisexual. Or neither. But August and I are hidden in the Forest, and we're worlds away from home, and I decide I don't have to answer my own questions right now. I don't have to do anything but keep August in my arms.

After what feels like an eternity, he pushes me away, brow furrowing. "But don't you think we're moving too fast?"

"August. Listen to me. In a place like this, it's now or never. I would prefer it if it were now, though."

That seems to soothe his thoughts. He screws his eyes shut, and I watch as his breathing slows.

In the darkness, his bruises look worse, his skin now more purple than any other colour. On each arm, there are great violet welts that don't do anything but deepen as time passes. Against his skin, they are grotesque, but I can barely remember what he looked like without them.

Rain beats against the canvas roof, streams of water running down the outside, droplets dripping inside. The diffused light of the fire shines through the rain, throwing dappled flickers onto the wet cloth. The sides of the tent ripple against the sudden wind and strain against the rope and pegs, the edges flapping wildly, feeling flimsy.

Ansel and Gracie soon come barrelling in, deciding that the heat of the fire isn't worth standing in the rain for. August and I shuffle to one side of the tent. It's dark and cramped, so it's less obvious that our arms are still wrapped around each other.

"Did you read the book?" Gracie asks through chattering teeth and pushes wet hair back from her face. Her cheeks are flushed and a droplet trails down her nose.

I shake my head, retrieving the book from the picnic basket. The fire leaves us with enough light to continue reading. Ansel takes the book from my hands and reads a random page aloud.

"When reaching death, some humans can find themselves in a personal heaven, identified by them reliving happy memories in their separate world. It is suggested that they move along the axis mundi from one happy memory to another."

"What's that?" Gracie asks, peering at the pages.

"The axis mundi? It's the cosmic axis, kind of like a connection between worlds." He pauses to find his place on the page. "Most people cannot leave their own 'heaven', although a practical application of string theory suggests that there may be a way to leave."

"What's that?" Gracie asks again.

"There's a lot of suggesting going on here," I comment.

"Shut up. I'm just reading the book." Ansel sighs, angrily flicking to the next page, but his damp fingers stick them together.

"Well, skip to the good parts."

Another sigh. "Fine. However, a personal heaven

is not exclusive to those who have died: people who are close to death may share their heaven—similar to purgatory—before moving on to their own. Most people who have avoided death have claimed that their shared afterlife was a Forest."

That's the part that catches our attention.

Ansel continues. "A Forest represents an unexplored realm full of the unknown. It stands for the unconscious and its mysteries. The Forest has a great connection with the symbolism of a nurturing figure as it is a place where life thrives. However, the addition of paper derives from the idea of a paper town: a fake town created by mapmakers to protect their copyright. As this Forest cannot be proven to be real, it can be identified as a Paper Forest."

Ansel abruptly stops reading and hurls the book against the side of the tent, narrowly avoiding Gracie's head. He stumbles to his feet and storms out into the rain, muttering curses he should be too young to know beneath his breath. Gracie crawls over to August and silently nestles into his arms. The firelight catches tears sliding down her cheek.

While August comforts her, I search the book for answers, not with a specific question in mind.

The writer has no explanation for Gracie or how she can claim to know so much about a place she's never been. I decide she must be a child whose imagination is so strong it leaks into reality, manipulating how the word functions. If she's scared and thinks monsters are lurking in the trees, her imagination will mould the surroundings until they're real but also unrealistic, fitting into a child's warped fantasies. If she's bored with walking and wants a change of scenery, all she has to do is think and a brook will appear by our side, a campfire will have built itself to warm her hands, and a tent will assemble to become her shelter throughout a storm. If she wills a body to come back to life, it might just do that.

Although the book has no explanation for Gracie, it does hold answers to the map. All of August's predictions are correct, and the matching handwriting proves it. In addition to that, the book explains that there is a way out: it exists in the circle between the two squares. It almost sounds too good to be true. But we can't think of our own way to escape our Paper Forest, so we're willing to believe anything that we're told.

EIGHT
AUGUST

The three of us lie together in the tent, silent, caught up in our own daydreams. I curl on my side with my back to the others, fingers tracing my lips at the memory of Oliver's kiss by the brook, the imaginary butterflies fluttering across my vision, red like warning signs. I try not to be swallowed up whole by the Catholic guilt that haunts my fond feelings and white lies, but the years of hating myself are part of me now. This is wrong. It feels wrong. But it's the only thing I have left.

As I remember fingers tangling in my hair and

my hands exploring skin, Oliver's face is replaced by someone else.

In my daydream, I'm seven years old.

I'm standing by the chain link face at the edge of the school playground with my best friend, re-enacting scenes from *Titanic*. I always play Jack while they play Rose as they have the same red hair, then they climb the fence and balancing on it like Kate Winslet on the back of the ship. I hold a wood chip up to my mouth and pretend to puff on it like a cigar before tossing it off the side of the 'ship' into the 'sea'. I fall to the ground as my best friend cries, "I'll never let go," and we pretend the end-of-lunch bell is a siren on the sinking ship. We jump from the fence one more time together, then race back each other back to the classroom although we're hand in hand, never letting go.

We're still hand in hand on the way home and the boys from school follow us to shout insults from across the street, waving angry fists and angry slurs, but this was a few years before they started throwing punches over words. My best friend whispers to ignore them, and we're in our own world as soon as we sneak in through the garden gate and hide amongst the cluster of hydrangea bushes furthest away from the house. They kiss my cheek, just to see what it feels like. I kiss theirs in return because that's what best friends do, isn't it?

The three of us lie together in the tent, almost silent, caught up in our daydreams. I hum *Hallelujah* beneath my breath and count my knuckles like a rosary, digging bitten nails into the skin, white bursts of pain blocking boyish features from my brain.

I wonder how much longer I'll punish myself before I accept that I have to live with this feeling, no matter how wrong it feels. It's the only thing I have.

NINE

Gracie leads us to our next destination, across the dried-out lake bed and back into the trees. She holds the map in her grubby hands, careful not to smudge any of the charcoal even more. We all have the shapes committed to memory, but now there's a golden trail that curves across the cloth, marking the path that it's chosen for us to follow. It only appears when the map is in Gracie's hands.

"Has anyone thought about what would happen if we died here?" Ansel asks. His arms are folded, and I can't tell if he's cold or if he's trying to cover up how the burn mark on his arm has started to spread across his chest and up his throat.

"No. Have you?"

The trees are veiled in mist, their trunks sombre brown with cracks that gnarl the bark. The mist wraps around like a blanket, the everyday unfamiliar sights of the Forest becoming mysterious, looming out at us in their whitened haze at the last moment like images from a half-forgotten dream.

"Of course I have. The book said that this Forest is a personal heaven. Does that mean that we're just our souls right now? Are we attached to our physical bodies anymore? Why has it grouped all of us together?"

I hold out my hands in front of me and watch as they become partially obscured. The sounds of birdsong that we once heard filling the air have stopped. Even our footsteps have been muffled by the mist. "You've thought about this way too much."

He sighs, irritable. The longer he stays in the Forest, the faster it consumes the likeable parts of his personality. "You haven't thought about it enough. If we die here, we could wake up in the real world alive and well. Or we could die and fade from existence forever."

August appears out of the mist and walks by my side. His hand slips into mine. I squeeze it tight, then say, "Or we could completely skirt around the subject of death and focus on finding the way home, couldn't we? It looks like there's a clearing coming up."

There is a clearing, but it isn't just a break from the trees.

A blanket of clouds fills the sky, smothering out the half-light until we are plunged into near blackness. The temperature drops a few degrees, and goosebumps rise on my arms. The chill creeps further up my spine as the fog parts to reveal a sea of bones as far as I can see.

"Well, this is a pleasant change of scenery," I mutter, dropping August's hand.

He chokes back a laugh.

Ansel glares at us. "Are you being serious right now?"

"Actually," I say, looking out across the bones, "I was being sarcastic."

The closest skeleton looks fresh. In some places, there is a pink sheen where the flesh has been inexpertly removed. Tool marks have gouged into recently living bone and left a round hole in the skull's forehead. The rear of the head has been cleaved open and is now hollow. The femurs have been sliced open and the marrow removed. This person can't have died peacefully: they were murdered.

August stamps his foot on a bone to see if it's brittle enough to break, and Gracie chooses this moment to vomit in the nearest bushes. Ansel runs to comfort her, but that won't help the fact that a child shouldn't have to see this much death.

Most of the skeletons aren't so fresh. The one thing they have in common is that they're all the bones of children, ranging from kids smaller than Gracie to teenagers the size of me. The bones are a graveyard for the visitors who didn't survive the Forest. It's a reminder that we are all made of flesh that can rot and bones that can be broken.

"If there are this many who are dead, how many do

you think are alive?" August asks. He pushes bones out of the way with the toe of his shoe to reveal more buried underneath. A lot of the skeletons are still dressed in a mixture of shorts and vests or warm winter clothes, some even with hospital gowns. I resist the urge to take something for myself.

I wonder with August. There must be hundreds, maybe even thousands, of skeletons in this clearing—a warning of how many lives the Forest has taken. There's no way of telling when the first skeleton was laid to rest, but it's easy to assume that there are still some alive, hidden away in the trees. We can't be alone in this Forest.

That's when I notice a teenage girl standing a few feet away from us, her presence obscured by shadows cast by the trees. Well, a teenage girl with transparent skin, standing in a pool of smoke. The first time I saw her, I wouldn't have noticed her if the Forest seen through her body wasn't a charred skeleton of reality. Now, the landscape seen through her skin is full of real skeletons, and they shake and quiver as if they never died. The smoke makes no sound, and it only parts to swallow up her feet as she drifts across the Forest floor, careful not to disturb the dead. Broken bones tremble from under the skin of the mist.

No one else appears to have noticed her. They're occupied with other things: Gracie vomits, Ansel comforts her, and August rummages through the bones as if he can find a sign of how they died. I rub hard at my eyes and, when I look again, the smoke girl is still standing a short distance away from me. Her eyes meet mine for a moment before her body dissolves and evaporates into smoke. I blink, and then she's gone.

But the pool of smoke remains on the ground, and it floats towards me.

I hear August shout my name as a dozen hands reach out of the smoke, grab my ankles, and pull me under.

I strain against zip ties, blood running over the plastic, red on white. My nose fills with the musty scent of the sack that covers my head, and my eyes strain for some sign of what is to come. It's not tied on tightly, so I wriggle and writhe until it's loose enough to slip off.

I sit up and take in my surroundings, wanting to rub at my swollen, tear-crusted eyes. They're so tender that it hurts to blink. In the darkness, I can almost make out the features of the room. The floor is stone, dark and worn smooth with age, and the only light comes from a dimmed old-fashioned lantern hanging from the centre of the ceiling.

Other than the muffled sound of voices in the distance, the room is a silent box. The air that was once stale and smelt of sewage also smells like human faeces. I crane my neck, trying to catch a glimpse of a door or a window, but there is none. For all I know, I could be deep underground in a handmade prison. I want to scream, but the gag in my mouth makes it difficult.

I can't remember much since they grabbed me in the graveyard of bones. Whatever they used to take me made my memory hazy. But I do remember one thing, and that memory comes flashing back as soon as I spot the corpse lying beside me. The only things that suggest she is dead are her blue-tinged lips and the burning red welts across her throat.

I remember two boys dragging her into the room while she was kicking and screaming, sounds smothered by something wedged inside her mouth. They threw her onto the floor, and she curled into a ball instead of trying to run, long, dark hair stuck to her damp cheeks and blood streaming from a gash on her forehead.

One boy stepped out of my line of vision, and I assumed he left the room through an exit I couldn't see. The other leaned over the girl, fumbling for something at his waist. I squinted and caught the glint of a belt buckle in the lantern light.

"We know you didn't come here alone, Catherine. There are always four. Where are the other three? Where are your friends, Cathy?"

She whimpered and shook her head frantically as he took a step forward, raising his hand as if to strike her. She flinched before he made another move and shuffled back towards the corner I was slumped in. Her eyes widened when she saw me, a silent plea for help.

I could've helped her.

I didn't.

I didn't want to see what happened next, so I screwed my eyes shut, counting down until it was all over. It became a countdown to when he snapped and decided to kill her.

First, he cuffed her arms and legs with zip ties, binding her mouth fully until her sobs became silenced. He taunted her from a distance for what felt like hours before the other boy stepped out from the shadows and glanced her way, peering down his nose with a crooked little smile.

"I'd offer you a drink, Catherine, but you seem somewhat tied up right now."

He slipped a dagger from his waistline and held it to her throat, pressing until she had a pearl necklace of blood droplets. She whimpered as he asked her, "What happened to your friends, Catherine? Where are they?"

She didn't reply. She couldn't. He dropped the dagger while the other boy looped the belt around her neck and pulled it tight, strangling her while she was still by my side. The sound of her choked final cry for help echoes in my thoughts.

As soon as the boys left, I pressed my hands against her chest as if I could bring her to life again, but I'm not like Gracie. There wasn't even a spark. Instead, I pounded against the walls and tried to cry out, but the only response was the echo of my voice. After that, I fell asleep and woke up gagged with bound hands. Now, I huddle in the corner, crying out in my mind for my mother, my siblings, and even August. I consider praying to a god I don't believe in. But no help comes. The next time someone walks into this room, nothing good will happen to me. Not even Gracie can imagine a way to save me.

With no natural light in the room, the space feels claustrophobic. I struggle to my feet, somehow grateful that my hands were bound in front of me. I stumble towards a door behind me that was obscured in shadows and throw my shoulder against it, shouting through the gag for someone to let me out.

No one answers. No one comes. And, after a while, my side aches, and I'm panting with frustration and fear. I don't know what these people could want from me. They must want it desperately enough to kill for it.

I settle myself back onto the floor, but it's impossible to find a tolerable position. All I can do is wait, my ears sharp and ears alert for the sound of footsteps outside the door, for a warning that someone is coming for me.

But the waiting is endless.

And the pain is endless.

And, for a moment, I want to hurt under my own conditions.

I hold the end of the zip tie between my teeth and pull it as tight as possible, wincing as the plastic cuts deeper into my skin, ignoring the beads of blood forming on my wrists. When it's tight enough that I start to lose feeling in my fingers, I lift my hands above my head and bring them down quickly into my stomach.

The tie breaks at its weakest point.

I lie for a second, gasping, rubbing at the welts around my wrists, blowing on the skin as if my breath can cool the burning beneath the surface. The pain feels comforting, but it is nothing compared to the pain of my death. And I just need to hurt more to feel alive—to feel real—again.

Within a heartbeat, I'm sitting at the edge of Catherine's bloodstain, holding the dagger they held against her throat, turning it over in my hands. It's small with a sharp blade and leaf green stones embedded in the hilt. As I run the blade along my palm, the edge barely breaking the surface, I think about a familiar feeling. I think about the way my sisters and I used to write messages on each other's skin with our fingers, telling stories no one else could hear.

I stretch out my arm and bring the blade down.

I have no way of telling how much longer I'm in the room, Catherine's non-rotting corpse by my side, my blood trickling into hers. My mind wanders, and I find it thinking about my family. The images are so detailed, so vibrant, that it feels like I'm part of them, like they could be real too.

Usually, in a counselling room with a circle of chairs, you would expect to find a group of teenagers, just like me and August and Ansel. We would have empty eyes, slumped postures, and minds that told us we were immune to the influence of society. Now, we all know that's not true: we are the most easily influenced. This room is full of adults, holding on to each other as their final shreds of hope flicker before them.

A man is standing at the edge of the circle, middle-aged and potbellied. His head is balding, but he has a neatly trimmed beard he scratches at. "We'll go around the circle one by one," he says, his voice creaky as if he smokes a pack of cigarettes a day. "Introduce yourself and tell us a little about why you're here, as much as you're comfortable sharing. Remember, we're here to support each other, not to block each other out."

The first person to stand is my mother. She's only in her late forties, but now she looks many years past her age. She has the delicate features of a porcelain doll, but her tears smear her hastily applied makeup, and her skin looks many sizes too big for her skinny frame. She smells of the cheap floral perfume—lavender— that my stepfather bought her last Christmas, but it barely covers the smell of her cigarette smoke. *My* cigarette smoke. My stepfather is sitting beside her. The only thing about him that looks different is that his moustache hasn't been trimmed. He doesn't stand.

"I'm Caroline Harwood. This is my husband, Michael. My son...*Our* son...His name is Oliver. He's in a coma. He's only seventeen."

Her hands shake as she talks, but her voice doesn't falter. Her words sound rehearsed, almost as if she's been repeating the same story over and over again to other counsellors, private therapists, or distant family who asked where I was when they came to visit on my brother's birthday. Michael reaches up and holds one of her hands in both of his, squeezing it three times.

"He overdosed on heroin a few weeks ago, and the doctors aren't sure if he's going to make it. He's still on life support. We're praying for the best, but it isn't looking promising."

A few tears leak out of her eyes as she sinks back into her chair, not uttering another word for the rest of the session. I want to comfort her, brush away her tears and whisper an apology into her ear, but I can't. The only thing that will comfort her is finding a way back home and sparing her from the pain of losing another child.

The counsellor continues around the circle, all the wet cheeks and hollow eyes blurring into one figure, looking like despair has been personified.

There's a young man with Gracie's dark hair and curious eyes, and I decide he must be her older brother. She was left critically injured at age seven—along with her mother—in a car accident where he was driving. Ansel's grandparents are there to speak about him, and I see echoes of his soft features in their faces. A middle-aged man and woman, who don't make eye contact or acknowledge each other's presence besides interrupting each other, talk about August. He doesn't look like either of them, and it sounds as if they're making up a story in the moment, fumbling over the details of a cancer diagnosis and a life expectancy that's about to expire.

After allowing each child to be spoken about for a few minutes, the counsellor steps in, sensing that the adults are becoming too distraught or too uncomfortable to continue. He stands in the centre of the circle and cracks his knuckles.

"One thing that you all have in common is that you have a child who is on the verge of being taken away from you, whether it is by a natural illness or something that could've been prevented. You mustn't worry, for they have been placed in the best hands and there are people who are trying their best to look after them."

Our family members lean in, and it's a moment that feels too intimate for me to witness. They're desperate to hear anything that could ease their pain, even if it's just a story woven for their own comfort. In this situation, it is more than a story, but it's one that I would give anything for it to not be real, for the truth behind each uttered word to disappear.

"While your children and grandchildren are away, I like to think that they're visiting a fantastic place, somewhere where they aren't restrained by an illness or held back by their own emotions. I like to believe that they're in a place called the Paper Forest, where there is nothing but health and happiness to greet them."

When I wake up, I'm in another dream. Maybe not a dream, but a vision: I'm watching the world through August's eyes.

He's holding Gracie's face between his hands, begging her to keep looking at him, not at the *thing* that's behind them. Ansel is laying on the ground, clutching at the burns around his throat, his body shaking like a seizure. Over Gracie's head, I catch flashes of it: a tall, sinewy thing, but not human—maybe once, but no longer. Not with those unnaturally long fingers tipped with broken claws, and not with shrivelled white skin that looks like crumpled paper. Not with that distended jaw hanging open to reveal cracked bloodstained teeth. Not with those eyes, milky and tinged with blue. And definitely not with a knife buried in its stomach up to the hilt.

The creature pushes a gnarled hand against its abdomen, grasping at the knife, panting through those broken brown teeth as it looks at August—*looks* at him with such hatred that he can't move. All he can do is beg Gracie to close her eyes and think of a happier moment as it stumbles forward and scrapes its claws down his back. He doesn't scream, just squeezes his eyes shut and clenches his jaw until I hear one of his teeth crack.

He keeps holding Gracie's face as the creature surges backwards, blood running down its claws as they pull out of his skin, flesh hanging off the tips like minced meat. I—*we*—risk a glimpse over the shoulder, taking in the scarring around its mouth as though someone sewed it shut and ripped it open again.

I don't get to look for long before a second monster leaps out of the trees and sinks its claws into August's ribs.

TEN

I wake up, missing the end of the dream, but the two boys have returned. They don't stop to talk and don't respond when they cut my gag, and I demand they answer my questions. They drag me out of the room, skin stained with tears and Catherine's blood.

Faded light shines through wintery branches, shadowy arms stretching across ancient ruins, illuminating the precious secrets of the Forest. The columns are the only complete thing amongst the worn and crumbling stone, the decay the only marker of time in a place of uncounted days. What is left stands despite itself, precariously defying gravity. Yet, this place, kept hidden by the trees, is safe.

The boys stand on either side of me, their hands gripping tightly on my arms to stop me from running away. Even if I knew where I was or how to find the others, or if I had any strength left in me to run, I wouldn't be able to escape. These ruins are from a castle designed to be a fortress.

The vast corridors of the castle are a playground. Everywhere I look, there are children, some younger than Gracie. A group of small boys nearly runs me over as they chase after an even smaller one, screaming inventive curses and carrying short swords that look too sharp for only a game. Girls who can't be any older than thirteen or fourteen lounge against the walls, some smoking sweet-smelling cigars on piles of thick furs. One of them is humming a song that nobody knows beneath her breath as another sways to the melody.

"Where do they come from?" I ask, mostly to myself. It's impossible to think that this many people are in one place when I've spent days with just the group as my company. It makes me wonder how many people are roaming through the trees.

The boy on my left laughs with the slight wheeze you get from years of smoking. "Same place you did."

We keep walking, and I keep looking around. The youngest kids I see barely come up to my hip, and the oldest are in their late teens. Death isn't that picky with who it takes.

I'm led into a large room like a ballroom with windows covered in translucent maps and a throne at the far side. A *throne room*. The boys drop my arms and I walk alone towards the throne. It's carved of fine dark oak, crested with jewels and decorative metals forming an elegant coat of arms for a kingdom that may no longer exist. Although it's an impressive throne, the thing that stands out the most is the young girl who sits on it, no older than Gracie, with a rusty and bloodstained crown perched on her head. There's a small patch of metal on her arm, no bigger than a coin. It ripples then clones itself, layering over the neighbouring skin like scales. I blink, and then it's gone.

The girl doesn't say anything when I approach her. Instead, a teenage girl steps forward to greet me. Her tangled ebony hair is adorned with rainbow leaves and her white dress—styled like a short toga—is surprisingly clean. She holds a bow in her left hand with the same care that you would give a baby. Scars cover every inch of her dark skin besides her face, but they're a metallic cobweb, silver and gold, rather than red and flesh tones. She looks like a lost warrior, beautiful and dangerous, emitting an aura of regality. It looks like she should be the one on the throne.

No one speaks, so I choose to. "Why would you wear an iron crown? It's tarnished. At least gild it so the outside looks gold."

There's a glimmer in the dark girl's amber eyes, and I think I spot her lips curl into a hint of a smirk, but it's gone in a second. "I apologise that we do not carry gilding materials around. We are unprepared, unlike you appear to be, but you also appear to not have a crown."

I'm too shocked by the joke to say anything.

She continues. "My name is Porcelain Castellan. This is Lilac Bonneville, the Queen and leader of the people living freely in the Forest." The girl on the throne shows no sign of acknowledgement, only adjusts how the crown sits on her head. The metal girl—Porcelain—continues, "We are establishing a life for ourselves here. All attempts to leave have been futile to this day." She speaks with a strong accent, thick and authoritative. "We would like it if you and your friends will stay with us."

"It's a shame that my friends and I have found a way to leave, isn't it?" I say, trying to sound more confident than I am. I have no intention of staying in a place like this for longer than I have to, not when I come out gagged and bound and covered in someone else's blood. And it's not a lie: we know there must be a way home. We just don't know what it is or what it will take to get there.

Porcelain's expression remains unfazed and amused. Lilac's brow furrows into a scowl, and she appears meaner than I've ever seen from anyone else her age. She still doesn't speak.

"All attempts to leave have been futile to this day," Porcelain repeats slowly, not losing her composure. "And you can believe me when I say that I have been in this Forest long enough to witness countless attempts."

Then I realise what it is that I hear in her voice. It isn't distance or foreignness: it's age, an age that stretches back to the beginning of this world.

Porcelain's eyes narrow. "I am aware that you were once given the option to choose a side, willingly or forcefully. You and your friends denied going willingly and chose to murder some fine soldiers. You caught our attention with that choice, and we wanted to have a discussion."

Soldiers? This is more than just a bunch of kids playing dress-up in a castle. This is a group of kids building a mechanical army. But what are they preparing to fight against? Why are their bodies melded into metal? I don't have the time to think of a response before Porcelain continues.

"Children like Lilac—like your Gracie—are special because they have the power to control the Forest. This power means that we also need to control them in order to protect the people. You may have met Catherine earlier. She knew another special child and refused to bring them to us for the guidance that they need."

I screw my eyes shut at the memory, but the image of her corpse flashes on the inside of my eyelids. I wonder if that will soon become Gracie's corpse.

"They have an illness that may occur once in their life, or come and go, or be triggered by stress. It is a rare psychological condition. In the Otherworld, the symptoms can include paranoia, hallucinations…" She lists other symptoms as if she's been rehearsing. "Here, it means that the thoughts inside their head escape into reality, and this makes them dangerous to us and themselves."

Some of the words sound familiar to me. "Hallucinations…Isn't that like schizophrenia?"

She nods slowly. "It is very similar to many of your Otherworld illnesses and disorders, but the power that the Forest holds alone manages to control many of the symptoms. Although children who have these conditions are becoming rarer with each group of arrivals, they can still do incredible damage to anyone or anything they have contact with."

There are more people in the Forest. Not just me and the others. Not just the people living in this ruined castle. There are more people than just us, a world's worth of people.

"If Gracie is so special," I begin, my voice faltering. I can't think of an answer to the unspoken question, so I have to ask. "Why did you make me come?"

Porcelain hesitates for a moment as if she also doesn't know the answer. "We need more recruits. Gracie is special, but she is young and will not understand what we are asking of her yet. It will be better coming from someone she trusts. Ansel is too weak, both mentally and physically. And your August will not be alive for much longer."

My August. My heart throbs. I wonder how biology can explain the physical pain in my chest when all I want is to keep him safe.

"How do you know that?" I remember the brief

conversation when Ansel told us how he daydreams about his death. August told us about his terminal cancer. He knew it could be the last day of his life at any point. This was the day we found out his name: not after the month, but after the Roman emperor.

"His bruises. Have you noticed them? They get worse every day and match the bruises found on his body in the Otherworld. It is more than just the cancer that is killing him."

"Is it?" I remember how I saw the bruises on our first day together and thought that he would be beautiful in another world. Now, the bruises are a sign of his upcoming death.

Then I remember his exact words from another moment.

I'm seventeen, not born in August. I have a brain tumour the size of a golf ball and it could be the last day of my life soon, but that's not why I'm here. I guess you'll have to wait and find out.

"This is a conversation you will need to have with him rather than me. The purpose of this conversation is that we're looking for a warrior. We have many soldiers, but we need a true warrior to join our ranks."

I choke back a laugh. "I don't want to join you. I don't want to be a warrior. I have no desire to do either of those things." I sigh. "I just want to go home."

There is no sound in the throne room, although I can see the people moving at the edge of my vision, moving but not talking. We become knee-deep in silence. No one speaks, so I allow my eyes to drift back to the throne.

Lilac wears a watch on her right wrist, not a colourful plastic one made for children, but an expensive one where the gold glints casually in the fading sunlight behind a circle of cracked glass. It's broken, but she still glances at it when no one's looking. I wonder if it belonged to a family member from her past life or a friend she made in the Forest. If she's holding on to a broken watch, it must have sentimental value, a way of keeping someone's memory alive.

That's when I realise that the child sitting on a too-large throne wearing a bloodstained crown is nothing more than that: a child. One with an imagination strong enough to change the world, but still a child. A lost one, too.

Lilac catches me staring at her watch. She repositions her crown and sits up straight, looking directly into my eyes. "All of us here respect your decision." She nods thoughtfully, as if she's plotting something. "I'll tell my guards to release you, then you should start running as fast as you can."

Lilac keeps her promise.

The two boys who escorted me into the throne room lead me out of the castle, joking between themselves, but they quickly slip into a language that sounds older than time itself, and I struggle to understand what they're saying. I assume that they're laughing at me.

Before leaving, they hand me a sword. The handle is bound in black leather, the hilt is decorated yet understated, and the blade is short. It's a lot heavier than it looks. I still know little about swords, but I'm certain that one like this will be of no use for protecting myself against monsters as an inexperienced fighter like myself.

And I need protecting.

A monster is waiting for me as soon as I'm deep enough into the Forest that I can't turn back and run to safety.

A tangle of limbs unfolds itself from the undergrowth, and the monster shrieks with all the pain and fury that I hold inside me. It's made of curses and corpses, a torso lined with more rows of ribs and spines than nature should allow, protruding eyeballs blinking rapidly between sinew. Claws the size of my arm bones curl around an ancient oak and split it into two as it heaves itself upright.

I turn around, and there's already another monster waiting behind me. What could have once been a human face opens up from the bottom of its jaw and around to the nape of its neck, revealing teeth smeared with what I can only assume is blood and rot. I faintly register the monsters hissing as if they're speaking to each other and another rustles in the undergrowth, but that doesn't matter. The only thing that matters is the third monster towering above me, dripping decay and blocking the only path.

My breathing becomes erratic. I try to fight it. I fight the feeling of being out of control as my body writhes to be free or shut down entirely, and I fight the feeling of dying all over again. It dawns on me that I was only dragged into this situation because Gracie is valuable—no, she's a threat—to the Forest. She is the one designed to be a weapon, yet I'm the one fighting to protect her.

As the monsters close in, I know that I'm outnumbered. I catch the shapes of smaller monsters emerging out of the trees, and I remember I don't have the skill to fight, even if the numbers were fair. But they're bigger than me, and they move slowly, and the density of the trees bordering the path in this part of the Forest is enough to restrict their movement.

I do the only thing that I know how to do.

I drop the unwieldy sword, and then I run.

My feet slip outwards on damp leaves as I race off

the path and into the depths of the Forest, freezing my throat as I gasp for breath. I stumble over a sharp rock, and then a jarring pain shoots from ankle to knee, then knee to hip. My fingers curl into sweaty fists, swinging forward as if it will make me run faster. I hear the monsters hissing from behind, but I don't risk turning around to see how close they are.

I can't run forever, so I veer to the left and hide, using the undergrowth as my cover. I stumble forward and fall onto something soft. Fabric scratches under my fingernails. Clothes. Clothes on a human body. I've fallen on someone. Or what used to be someone.

The stench of rot is everywhere. I look down at the bloated face. The body is undeniably human. A teenage girl, painfully thin, her inky black hair worn like the mane of a lion. There's a hospital bracelet around her fragile wrist: *Jemima Fowler*. Patches of her skin are burned down to the bone, black and red, bubbles rising like lather on a bar of soap where the burns are worse. The skin on her mottled face is stretched so tight it's split apart, leaving white slashes of naked bone poking through the gaping wound. She can't have died from natural causes.

But I can't think about her right now. All I can do is to be glad that I'm not her and pray that the monsters don't find me.

I stay hidden amongst the bushes beside her body. My heart aches as I lean against damp wood with only one sound to be heard: the sound of my pulse throbbing in my throat. The silence suddenly surrenders to the scream of footsteps approaching me. A narrow stream of moonlight fills little areas of the ground like spotlights, and I catch a glimpse of a shadowed figure quickly avoiding the brightness.

I hold my breath. Each second plays on for an eternity as I crouch perfectly still, listening to each footstep. It doesn't sound like another monster, but it could be one of the mechanical soldiers.

Then familiar blue eyes fill my vision, and I allow myself to give into my fear.

Instead of fragile euphoria, I am drained mentally and physically, the tension growing in my face and limbs, reminding me of the feeling I had whenever my chosen substance of the night entered my bloodstream. With the slightest of smiles and pink puffed eyes, I reach out my hand and allow August to pull me out of the undergrowth and into his arms. Ansel and Gracie watch from a distance.

I press against him, mouth opening under his, arms wrapping around his neck. He runs his hands down my sides, over my hips. My hands slip down and mould to the shape of his shoulder blades, the curve of his body beneath his ribcage, thumbs arching over raised ridges of fresh scars across his back. Then words spill from his mouth: "Don't you ever leave me again."

Ansel coughs to clear his throat, and I pull away from August, slipping my hand into his instead.

"I have so much to tell you."

My story begins with the smoke girl and the dozen hands that pulled me into the ground, but I don't mention that it's the second time I've seen her, and no one else mentions if they've noticed her before. I talk about Catherine and the dark room next, the smell of blood flooding my senses at the memory. Then it's the ruined castle hidden within the trees and the children and teenagers from everywhere in the world. The Otherworld. Then it's Porcelain with her metallic scars and Queen Lilac sat on the throne wearing a bloodstained crown.

From there, I describe how she was looking for a warrior to protect her people from an unknown threat. I skip the part where I was offered the job. Gracie's eyes water when I tell her about how she's special, but she refuses to let any tears fall; it's shocking for her to discover how she's been manipulating the Forest, even if it hasn't been for the best. But she cries silently as her eyes drift to the handprint that continues to creep up Ansel's throat. She clutches the book to her chest as if it were a teddy bear.

I leave out the part about August dying and decide to end with the monsters and the corpse, and that brings me up to the present moment.

"We found you," Ansel states as soon as I've finished talking.

"I know. Thank you."

There's a brief pause. "Just so you know, we could've been out of here by now if your boyfriend wasn't obsessed with wanting to save you."

The comfort of August's presence doesn't last for long. I decide that shoving Ansel to the ground and punching him is a reasonable thing to do.

At first, there is guilt as he doesn't try to fight back, an attempt to stop, but I give in, realising how much I enjoy hurting his smug face. I hope that there's blood seeping beneath his skin, ribs fractured. I know that there's no doctor, no evidence, and I wonder if we might finally find out what happens when someone dies in the Forest.

With every hit, I feel a cold burst of delight, a buzz I can get no other way.

But the buzz feels familiar.

It feels like cigarettes and pills and heroin.

It feels like the reason I'm here.

August grabs my arms and drags me away. Ansel sits up, wipes the blood away from his nose with the back of his hand, and then stares at me. His eyes aren't full of fear or pain; they're full of anger.

ELEVEN

ugust and I lie together in the weeds, staring into the sky. We're alone; Ansel stormed off to avoid me and find out if anything of interest is nearby, and he took Gracie with him. I wouldn't want to be around me right now either.

With the sun half sunk, there are faint constellations in the darker part of the sky, and we take turns pointing out the ones we recognise and making up names for the ones we don't. I recognise the tattered band of the Milky Way with Sirius and Orion shining against the blackness. The Pole Star is overhead where the sunset meets the night, and the Great Bear hangs over the circle of this world. Beyond the crown of the setting sun are strange groupings of stars I haven't seen before, like a dagger-shaped group and a few crosses.

August is better than me at finding shapes in the sky, and he makes up stories to accompany each one. They remind me of the stories Rowan would tell to lull me to sleep, tales of gods and deities who had once conquered the world.

"That one looks like a fish." He pulls me close and points out a triangle attached to one end of a kite—six stars in total. "It's called Riba."

"What does that mean?"

He rolls his eyes as if it's obvious. "It means 'fish'."

"That's creative. What's the story behind the fish?"

He doesn't hesitate before he speaks. "Back in the days when people's lives still revolved around Greek gods, there was a sea nymph. She had a name with a lot of vowels in it that I can't pronounce, but it translates to 'Silvery One'. She loved a guy who transformed into a river. That must've upset her a bit because she drowned herself with the hope of turning into water, just like him. She didn't. She was a good nymph, and the gods loved her, so they preserved her spirit, making it into a constellation so everyone can remember her."

When he's finished telling the story, we return to staring at the sky. Most of the constellations and their positions are the same as they are at home, and the homesickness arrives in waves.

My vision softens with tears, melting the starry sky into a Van Gogh painting, everything bigger and brighter, blurring beautifully. The stars almost succeed in stealing every thought in my mind, leaving behind the images of blue eyes and strange marks on a map.

But I'm losing hope that we'll ever get home. Maybe I'll be trapped here forever, waiting to see whose real body will give up on them first out of the two of us, if the heroin will fatally slow down my nervous system before the cancer eats through him.

It's not something I want to think about.

A small part of me wonders why I'm trying to find a way home when I was so desperate to leave.

That's not something I want to think about either.

I roll onto my side so I'm face-to-face with August. "Have you ever cared about someone so much that you physically ached? It sucks. Especially when you know it can't last forever. Or that it probably shouldn't have started in the first place."

His eyes glint in the half-light. "Well, that didn't hurt at all."

"You know what I mean. If one of us survives or dies in the real world—the *Otherworld*, they call it—it's over, I guess. If one of us dies here, it's over. If we hadn't been dying in the first place, we wouldn't have met. And it hurts that this is how it is. We don't have a chance at a normal relationship."

"I think we're going to die here," he says.

"Me too," I say. "I try not to think about it."

I wind my fingers through his hair. It's thicker than mine and curlier, and it shines bronze in the light. There's a pattern of freckles across his cheek in the shape of Cassiopeia. He shuffles closer and rests his head in the crook of my neck, long hair tickling my cheeks. I resist the urge to twist it around each finger, pulling the curls straight and watching them spring back into shape. Instead, I watch as he closes his eyes and smiles like he's trying not to. I smile too, only because he isn't looking.

Something about the gesture makes me wish we had a chance at a normal relationship and were in my home together, curled up on the sofa in front of a fire, playing with each other's hair and exchanging kisses beneath blankets. We would be happy, but it's hard to imagine happiness when there's a chance my mother would be repulsed to see two boys lying together in her living room and my siblings might not understand why their older brother is kissing another boy. But maybe they'll understand and be accepting, and my imagined happiness can one day become real.

That's the one good thing about the Forest: I don't have to worry about how anyone else will react.

I contemplate my dream scenario for a while longer, feeling August's heartbeat against my chest and his breath on my neck, hyperaware of how alive he still seems to be. I keep imagining us together on the sofa and, when Gracie returns, I imagine her as one of my sisters walking in.

She walks over and sits beside us in the weeds. She's alone.

"Where's Ansel?" August asks, sitting up slowly. He reaches out to pick a stray twig out of her hair.

She frowns at him but doesn't bat his hand away. I guess the twig was intentional. "Ansel is gone."

"What do you mean?"

"We went for a walk because he's very angry that Oliver hit him, even though he deserved it for being mean. He asked if I could use the map to find my way back to you. I said yes, yes I could. He said—"

August sighs. "Gracie, where has Ansel gone?"

"He's gone to find the castle. He told me to tell you not to follow him."

"I guess we're going to have to follow him."

As we follow the golden trail on the map back to Ansel, it begins to snow.

There's no way to know which direction to go. Anything that could've been familiar is hidden behind a dense layer of whiteness. Even August, only a few steps in front of me, is little more than a crude outline of a person. The soft crystals find their way into my clothes and slip down my neck and stomach, turning my skin icy. I raise a hand to shield my eyes. The wind is ferocious, and the light reflecting off the ground is blinding. All I can do is bow my head until my chin touches my chest and continue walking.

We walk until the snow suddenly stops.

Well, it doesn't stop. We've walked into a perfect circle on the Forest floor that is free of snow, like being trapped in an invisible snow globe.

Gracie looks around, the amazement clear on her face. "Is this a fairy circle?" she asks, turning towards August. "Or is it a devil's circle?"

His brow furrows in confusion, then he scans the surroundings as if he's seen them before and nods in confirmation.

I run a hand through my hair as I look around,

tugging through tangles and freeing stray snowflakes. "What's a devil's circle?"

August doesn't know either, but he's a storyteller above anything else. I imagine the threads of a story weaving together in his mind. "Legend says that circles like this are the exact place where the devil himself can rise from the depths of Hell and come to Earth." His voice becomes low as if he's trying to keep the Forest from overhearing him. "It's at this place that the devil is supposed to walk in circles as he thinks up new ways of causing trouble for humanity. Sometimes, under the cover of night, he walks as he plots against good and on the behalf of bad. People try to camp in circles like this and wake up miles away. They try to stay awake all night to see the devil, but they always get lulled to sleep by a soft voice."

Gracie shudders before sitting down in the centre of a circle. She uses a broken twig to draw star shapes in the dirt, then what I assume is a self-portrait, then a recreation of the map. Then she goes back and adjusts her self-portrait until it looks something like a devil. I turn away.

Levitating a foot off the ground behind me is a pearly white object, glowing a hazy translucent blue. It's nothing more than a chill in the air at first, a shimmer of mist.

"Is that a ghost?" August asks with fear in his voice, as if this is the scariest thing we've encountered so far.

Through the ghost, the Forest becomes out of focus like a blurry photograph. It's like the soft susurration of the wind then, as it becomes clear, more sharply focused, I see a face that causes something to itch in the back of my brain. Images start flipping through my memory, disconnected, made-up pictures of things I've imagined but never had the chance to see, like drawings in a book.

The face belongs to my dead sister.

Her thick curls, doe brown eyes, and golden skin are exactly as I remember. She's wearing the simple patterned sundress she died in and has the rag doll tucked in the crook of her arm.

"Rowan?"

My older sister's eyes widen when she sees me. "Oliver? Is that you?" Her voice breaks as if she's on the verge of tears. "It can't be you. It's just the Forest playing tricks on me again."

I step towards her and reach out, but my hand passes straight through her arm—the skin evaporating like mist and then stitching back together where I make contact, living skin against the dead. She shudders at my touch and frantically steps away from me, but there's a small reassurance in the fact that we are at different stages of being dead. "You shouldn't be here."

In the corner of my eye, I see August take Gracie's hand and walk her to the opposite side of the circle, giving me a few moments alone with my sister's ghost. "I overdosed. You're the one who shouldn't be here."

"I died when I fell off the roof." Her tears start to fall. Her bottom lip trembles, but she bites it until it stops. "I woke up here, then I died here too."

And I'll die here too.

"Oliver, you have to understand something," she says. "The only rule of this place is that we each accept what brought us here."

"Why are you still here?" I question. By now, more shapeless ghosts are gathering around, their attention locked on me, the boy who's barely more alive than they are.

"I fell off the roof," she says again.

"And what is this place? This Forest. Heaven? Hell? Somewhere in between?"

"We don't know," she replies softly. "There's no rule saying we should know. It's not too bad here, though, once you get used to it."

That could be said for anywhere in the universe. I think of the monsters and the child soldiers and the girls made of metal. I realise that maybe my life might have been worth living after all.

Rowan drifts closer. She reaches out a hand as if to brush my hair out of my eyes, but she stops before her fingertips pass straight through me. Her face crumples. "You look so much older, Oli," she whispers. "You need to keep getting older. You need to leave this place."

Her image flickers in front of me and her brow furrows as if she's trying her best to stay, but it's not enough. Her lips move frantically. I can't hear what she's saying. Then she's gone. August appears in the spot where she was standing. His face is streaked with tears, but he still tries to smile.

"More of those soldiers are coming. We need to get out of here."

After seeing the ghost of my loved one, it's tempting to forget about Ansel, but Gracie insists we find him. She leads the way again; navigating us through the Forest takes her mind off what could have happened to Ansel and what is happening to her.

The Forest is beautiful in this moment. Trees stretch tall over our heads, and we step across a blanket of low ferns and moss that sounds like a whisper. All the colours are muted—everything is faded green or grey. Where the soil peeks through the undergrowth, it's pitch black. The ground is an uneven map of tree roots and holds in the earth. Light filters down through the leaves, bouncing and refracting off their unnaturally shiny surfaces, painting everything crisp and clear like a mirrorball. The only sounds come from us.

It's almost too quiet.

I breathe in deeply and listen.

No birdsong, no scurrying of small animals. No monsters or metallic teenagers. Not even the sound of the wind—the breeze is choked by the density of the trees. There's no sound, but there's an odour beneath the layer of clean air, mixed in with the decay of vegetation. It's a scent that's laced with death. Then I realise what kind of Forest we're in.

To the right, there's a handwritten sign half-obscured by the trees: *Your life is a precious gift from your parents.*

Then, to the left, in sloppily painted block capitals: *Please think about your parents, siblings, and children.*

August spots a sign in front of us and stops walking so he can read it. "'Consider the love of your family'. What kind of place is this?"

I take a breath. "It's the Suicide Forest."

August doesn't say anything, just shakes his head in defeat.

159

The revelation strips away the beauty of the Forest. It's returned to being a place of misery and mystery. I wonder how anyone can want to spend their last moments in the real Forest—Aokigahara—or if they get lured in with false breezes and sunlight and a mask of peace.

A few tense minutes pass before we see the first glimpse of what this version of the Forest truly is. Gracie gasps, but it's just a pile of scattered bones taken over by moss. It's hard to believe that the cracked ribcage and part of an arm once belonged to a living human being.

"It's okay," August whispers, mostly to her, partly to himself. He crosses himself subtly. Gracie screws her eyes shut as if it will remove the image from her mind, but it's already joined the memories of the other bodies that she's seen here.

There's another body only a few minutes away, a fresher one, still clothed in a threadbare Bon Jovi t-shirt and in mostly one piece. It's hanging against the trunk of a tree. We all try to keep our eyes trained on the path directly ahead, but I can see it in my peripheral vision, and I wonder if its rotting face will shift towards mine if I look for too long. I'm on edge and I feel as if the broken neck could jerk in our direction at any moment. It doesn't.

We walk onwards and try to resist the urge to run. I end up carrying Gracie in my arms so she can bury her face against my chest. There are bodies upon bodies hidden in the trees. Some are in piles and some are scattered in separate pieces. One dressed in a suit and boutonniere—ready for prom—lies against a fallen tree, jaw hanging open in a permanent scream. I want to reach back and take August's hand, but both of his are clamped over his mouth in shock.

We keep going through mile after mile of decomposing bodies before Gracie stops us. She untangles herself from my arms and stands with her hands on her hips. "We're going in circles," she insists.

"No, we're not," I say, even though I've been thinking the same thing for the last few minutes. She's right. She's always right, and we've also passed the first hanging body three times. The body looks bigger now, as if it's trying to become more noticeable, showing us we're going the wrong way.

I blink.

The corpse isn't bigger.

It's closer.

"It moved," Gracie whispers, grabbing onto the sleeve of my sweatshirt.

"Maybe not," I say, but I know it's not true. It wasn't in that spot before. "Maybe it's just your eyes playing tricks on you."

August appears by my side. He reaches out to stroke Gracie's hair. "We've been in this Forest for too long, that's all. Reality is bending."

But this is our reality now. Something behind us moves, shuffling through the undergrowth. We turn on instinct; it's the first noise the trees have made since we left the devil circle. There's nothing there. Whatever we heard isn't close enough to see. A few ferns might waver, but I can't tell if they really are or if it's my imagination.

"Turn around!"

Gracie's shriek burns into my mind as I turn again. The body has moved. It's at least four trees closer and this time it's facing directly at us. The decomposing eyes watch us with something that could be interest. The expressionless face is like a dare, practically eager, like a child on Christmas morning.

Behind us, the trees whisper again, but I don't turn to look. I've seen enough horror films to know what will happen. The next time I turn around, those empty eyes will be inches from my own.

"What should we do?" August whispers, even though I doubt the corpses are listening to us. They're simply watching, waiting for the right moment.

I shrug, watching Gracie stare down the nearest body. "Keep an annoyingly close eye on it, I guess. There's nothing we can do."

There's nothing we can do. This situation feels far too familiar and I know August feels it, too. "Last time, we fought them."

"But we don't have Ansel anymore, and we can't risk

163

anyone else getting hurt." The image of the handprint burnt into Ansel's skin fills my vision, alongside Catherine's corpse. Then Jemima Fowler's burnt body and the bones poking through the flesh of her swollen face. Then the body at the bottom of the ravine with the eyelids eaten away and insects burrowing through the skin.

August groans in frustration. He runs a hand through his hair, knotting strands around his fingers. "How far do you think we'll have to go for the Forest to change again? Could we run for it?"

I shrug again.

We run.

We run until the scenery changes from deciduous trees and fallen trunks overrun with moss to a bramble-filled meadow and pines. We run until we're haggard, bloody, and half on our knees. I collapse into the undergrowth, and August falls beside me, leaning in to tuck his head into the crook of my neck. Gracie stumbles more gracefully to the ground and curls into a ball next to us. Her eyes are screwed shut and I hear her counting quietly as her breaking slows down. A waterfall of tears drips down her cheek.

"I want my mummy," she whispers. She plucks a vibrant blue wildflower from the ground.

August wraps an arm around her. "So do I, buddy," he murmurs back. He takes her flower and weaves it into one of her braids.

They stay like that for a few minutes, August's arm around Gracie's shoulders, her head resting on his chest, listening to the erratic drum of his heartbeat. Then they're ready to go again. August pulls me to my feet and I pull Gracie to hers.

"Let's go home."

A few hours later, August starts to cough. He hacks continuously for a while before taking in a sharp gasp of breath that sounds like it's painful for him. At the end of each cough, there's a whistling sound as his airways close. They're coming thick and fast, and he's struggling to get enough air.

It's not just the cough that worries me—his body is now almost entirely black and blue with bruises. He must be dying faster than the Forest can heal him.

Exhaustion never affected us before, but now he tires as we walk. Gracie curls up by his side whenever we stop to rest. At one point, she presses her hands against his aching ribcage and wills him to get better, but nothing happens. The only thing she can offer him now is the comfort of her presence and her fingers running through his hair. In this moment, they look like brother and sister.

"You do realise I'm dying, right?" he says while I fuss over him for the hundredth time. It hurts me to hear what we both know is true.

I look away from him for a second. Gracie is standing out of earshot, and she stares at the ground, squinting in concentration. She raises a hand, and a small pink tent appears in front of her, then a larger khaki one big enough for a family. She raises her other hand, and the broken twigs on the ground turn into a campfire. She smiles at no one before disappearing into the pink tent.

August traces circles on the back of my hand and my gaze returns to him. "Yeah. I know. I just don't want to believe it."

He smiles sadly. "I guess it's time for me to tell you my tragic backstory."

"As much as I'd love the full version, could you give me a summary? I can't help but feel like we're pressed for time."

"Sure," he laughs, and it's still one of the most beautiful sounds I've ever heard. "I would like to welcome you to the first listening of the summarised life story of August Blaire."

August was born in late September in a small town in the south of England, one that he repeated the name of several times and I still couldn't quite catch it. His mother died from complications with his birth, and it took less than a month for his father to jump into a new relationship. August never figured out if that was how his father chose to mourn or if it was because he didn't want to handle a newborn baby on his own.

It took eleven years for August to start wondering why the face he saw in the mirror didn't match either of his parents: dark curls and brown skin versus straight, fair hair and faint freckles.

It was another year before the problems started.

When he was thirteen, August kissed another boy on the cheek after church, and a boy from school who saw hit them both before school the next day. When August got home, his stepmother would hit him too, a decade of maternal love disappearing at the first sign of a son who she claimed defied her god. When he went to bed each night with bloodshot eyes and tear-stained cheeks, he would watch as the bruises formed across his skin, warm brown turning to cold black and blue. He hasn't seen himself without a bruise since.

There were another few months of fists and taunts until his father kept him home from school to haunt his bedroom instead, endless weeks of loneliness occasionally disrupted by infrequent visits from his best friend. He taught them how to play chess, and they taught him how to sew patches over the rips in his jeans until the air turned warm and they taught him how to cut his jeans into shorts instead.

He tells me about conversion therapy again, but that's not the end of his bad memories.

The bloody black bruise of August's anger didn't fade with the seasons, or the scars, or the burn from the words that followed him through the daylight, and then he realised it was him who was being haunted. He woke up soaked in sweat at the memory of fists, and he lay there clutching at his bedsheets, as the shadows that lurked in the corners of his room melted into faces and the bruises became stained glass across his skin. And then he noticed it wasn't just his sexuality that was 'wrong' with him.

August was given his cancer diagnosis one month after his sixteenth birthday. His father tried everything he could to help: every type of chemo, every type of therapy, every type of experimental drug possible. He put his money into private healthcare until the banks stopped giving him loans to pay for it. Nothing could stop the monster from growing inside of his son's head and nothing could stop the bruises appearing across his son's skin, hidden beneath layers of clothing.

Just over one year later, August reached the final few weeks of his life expectancy, but he wasn't at the end. He was admitted to the hospital one night, unconscious, with bruises in the shape of fingertips across his throat.

It wasn't the cancer that killed him. It was his stepmother.

TWELVE

AUGUST

In my daydream, it's the summer before my twelfth birthday.

My best friend and I had a sleepover that lasted for weeks, tucked up together in my twin-sized bed, sneaking out to the field at the bottom of the hill after midnight in the moonlight. We'd wander the darkened high street, stopping at the all-night kebab shop for a portion of lukewarm chips to share between us for the rest of our walk.

And we'd lie together in the weeds at the base of the hill and count the glow of distant streetlights as if they were stars in the sky. My best friend would ask if any of them made constellations, and I would invent them in the moment, turning scattered amber orbs into animals and ancient gods. That was the beauty of constellations: the universe gave me stars, and I saw stories in them. Seeing purpose in the incidental made me realise just how lonely I was on the planet until then, desperately searching for meaning elsewhere in the universe.

But I wasn't lonely anymore, not with my best friend beside me. We were the only friend each other needed.

For the rest of the summer, we stayed up late and confessed our secrets to each other as we walked the streets, singing 'our song' to the shadows. Near the end of the summer, my best friend stayed home with me while I was grounded for throwing a rock through the church's stained-glass window. We snuck out to hold hands on the beach and sip milkshakes through striped paper straws, and the gentle night-time waves and the blinking of traffic lights was the soundtrack to our summer.

One night, instead of sneaking out to the field, we tucked ourselves together in the bottom of my wardrobe, kicking a suitcase with a broken handle and worn-out shoes onto the carpet.

"My dad's always mad nowadays," my best friend said, chewing at the skin around their thumbnail until it bled, looking a lifetime's worth of years younger than eleven.

I nodded as if I understood, but I was making a story instead. "I think your house is haunted. I've been meaning to tell you."

There was a moment of silence while they thought about it, and then they shrugged and sighed. Their dad really wasn't that bad, they thought. He came home smelling of weed and tequila, and he raised his voice when something in the house wasn't quite right, but he only hit them sometimes.

"I could live with my mum," they said, counting carefully across their fingers. "I haven't seen her in six months. *Seven* months. I hope she hasn't forgotten about me."

Both my best friend and I knew it was wishful thinking.

It was my turn to sigh next. "I found out that my mum is dead. My real mum. She died after giving birth to me."

My best friend raised an eyebrow but sat in polite silence. They'd been suspicious since they met me, wondering why I looked so different to my parents, but never figured out if it was adoption or an affair or something else that they shouldn't speculate about.

There was a moment when tears clouded my eyes, but I quickly blinked them away. I replaced the sadness with a smirk, looking a lifetime's worth of years older than eleven. "Maybe she's one of the ghosts in your house."

THIRTEEN

"So, in conclusion, I'm dying." August accompanies the grim fact with a sad smile, shifting slightly so his head rests in my lap.

My fingers weave into his hair, and I twist small sections of it into braids like I'm helping the twins get ready for school one more time. From here, I can see the faded acne scars across his cheeks. The penny-sized, penny-shaped birthmark above his collarbone. The white dot below his jaw that must have been from chicken pox when he was younger. The scratch on his neck—did I do that?

"What's your last wish?" I ask, reaching for one of his hands, rubbing my thumb across his palm. His skin is warm, too warm, almost feverish.

His eyes drift shut. "My what?"

"You know, your last wish. When people find out that they're going to die soon, they either go crazy and try to complete their entire bucket list, or they choose one big thing they want to do before they die."

He turns silent as he thinks. "I want you to dance with me."

We stand together, but he's shaking so much that I have to hold him up. There are no intricacies to the dance. It's just the two of us, arms wrapped around each other, swaying in time to the breeze. Our bodies are pressed together tightly, but my hands clutch at August's waist, moving restlessly as if I can pull him even closer. I find comfort in the pressure of his cool hand against the back of my neck and the sound of fallen leaves crunching with each tentative step. August sings under his breath, and I don't know what the song is, but it sounds like one of his stories: sad, but with a hint of hope.

I lose count of how many times I squish his feet under mine. Still, he smiles faintly, his sadness fading as I spin him around, watching as his curls fly out and bounce with each twirl. When I dip him, our gazes lock.

He's staring at me, eyes wide, shining in the half-light. It's a look of love and longing and terrible sorrow, and I feel it reflected in my own eyes.

It's too much.

I look away.

"Your eyes are different colours," he states, pulling himself back up onto both feet. My hands stay on his hips to keep him steady.

I shake my head. "They're both just brown."

"They're different browns." He grabs my face in his hands and tugs me down to his height, gazing intensely into my eyes. "The right one is green-brown, like olives. Like the leaves in this goddamn Forest. The left one is yellow-brown, just like caramel. Almost golden. That's my favourite colour."

And his eyes might just be mine.

August stands close enough for me to breathe in his scent. His arms wrap around my neck, and, in one gentle pull, our skin touches. I feel a hand in my hair, how he loves the softness, watching it tremble as he releases it. Then it moves down my cheekbones and towards my lips. He leans in to kiss me, and I tilt my head down to catch it. He's soft and warm, an early summer afternoon. My hands circle his back and, with a laugh, I lift him right off his feet, carrying him inside the empty tent, letting him fall with a small bounce on the sleeping bags Gracie provided. Our gazes meet for just a moment, just enough for us to feel safe with one another.

Then it's like I can feel the butterflies on my arms once more, the delicate touch of August's fingers trailing across my skin. There's the all-too-familiar ghost of a hand resting on my waist and my face and my chest. The gentlest kiss on my lips. It's as if I'm seven years old and playing in the garden, or fourteen years old and climbing the fence for a first kiss.

As if I'm seventeen years old and counting down the days until my last.

August's skin is dark amber in the firelight. The orange glow warms his skin from blue to brown, mahogany hair curling around his head in a crown. My fingers caress his jawline as if I'm afraid that a heavier touch could break him. With the bruises marking his body, he already looks broken. On skin as damaged as his, the fresh ones are harder to spot, and now he winces with pain from each movement.

I kiss him some more across his cheekbones. The moment sends me into a giddy haze, one that doesn't end until our bodies are still once more, warm and curled in as close as two souls can be. The bruise beneath my lips fades like the last petals of summer, kissed purple and yellow as the bronze hue of his skin returns. The bruises won't be gone forever, but they've disappeared long enough to give us a few moments of bliss.

When the stars stop spinning, August is lying in the curve of my arm. I'm gazing at him, head propped up on hand. He looks dazed. His eyes are half-lidded, tracing slow circles over my collarbone, then my neck, then across my jawline. His heart is still racing, slamming against mine. We lay there in comfortable silence, fingers across freckles on cheeks until Gracie comes to see us what feels like hours later, the book in her hands.

"I found something," she says, rapidly flicking through pages until she finds the one that she wants. She thrusts it towards us then sits cross-legged on the ground, her hands shaking with excitement.

On one of the last pages of the book, there is a crude drawing of a gate surrounded by notes: seven feet tall, iron, with a top that resembles the decorative roof of a religious building. There is no fence on either side, leaving the blackened catch dangling in mid-air as if it's resting on an unseen barrier. The writing beneath the drawing simply states 'Home'.

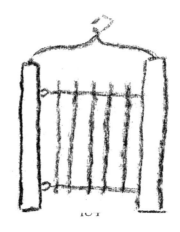

"Oliver." August clutches my hand. "We've found our way home."

Now that we know what we're looking for, it's even more tempting to leave Ansel to his fate so we can find our way home. We eliminate the possibilities for where the gate could be on the map until there are only a few markings left we haven't discovered. The map still has no way of telling time or distance, so we start walking towards what should be the closest of the marks and hope that it won't take what's left of our lives.

"Can I tell you a story?" Gracie asks August. She grabs his little finger in her fist and swings their joined hands between them as we walk.

"Sure," he smiles. He winces, and I know his bruises are back and worse than before. "What's it about?"

"Hansel and Gretel. Have you heard it before?"

He pauses in mock contemplation. "I might have, but I can't quite remember how it goes. Can you tell me the story again?"

Gracie beams. She retells the story, but it's not the simplified child-friendly version that Ansel once told her. "Hansel and Gretel were the children of a poor woodcutter. When a great famine settled over the land, the woodcutter's mean second wife took Hansel and Gretel into the woods and left them there so she and her husband wouldn't starve. She wasn't their real mummy, so she didn't care about them. Hansel and Gretel got kidnapped by a witch who ate people, even though she lived in a house made of cake."

I walk ahead of them until their voices fade.

Today, the Forest trees are thinner and it looks like there could be a clearing ahead. Half of the ground is submerged beneath murky water, and the other half is mud that I sink into past my ankles. It's a swamp. The ground soon gives way to a marsh full of tall reeds, the mud becomes firmer, and some of the water disappears. The remnants of the sunlight fall directly onto a giant fallen tree trunk we can use as a bridge. It isn't a dangerous drop, just a messy landing.

With a careful step, I test the bark. It's damp with

a covering of moss. It isn't too slippery, but it isn't like the firmer Forest floor that I've become used to. The trunk is wide, about three arm spans, yet the top is still deeply curved. I take a deep breath and go, eyes on my feet and the next few paces of the tree, arms stretched out like a tightrope walker. Steady. Steady. One step at a time until the other end of the tree appears.

A girl steps out of the reeds.

She walks alongside the tree, feet dragging through the water, looking so painfully normal at first that I can't believe that Gracie lets out a scream as the girl draws level with us.

Most of her back is gone: the skin, the muscle, the tissue. Claw marks tear through her flesh, skin and bone gouged out until the moonlight-white pillar of her spine is exposed. There's no blood, but her organs are exposed inside the cage of her torso. Another claw has sliced along the base of her skull. A thick black sludge bleeds from the injury.

I don't want to believe that she's still alive, but the ragged sound of her breathing comes into focus. There's no way that she can still be alive, but she's still walking, dragging a bloodied sweatshirt by the end of the sleeve. It catches around a reed, and she doesn't seem to notice as it slips from her fingers.

August covers Gracie's eyes so she can't see the girl, and I crouch down as close to the edge of the trunk as I dare so I can see her better. She keeps walking, not acknowledging us once, trudging through the mud until she reaches the edge of the marsh and disappears into the trees.

I hope she doesn't have to live in pain for much longer.

The silence behind me is suddenly replaced by a shrill scream. "Oliver, come here! August fell!"

My head snaps around in panic, but I see August is lying on the trunk, not submerged by the marsh. I run back to his side, less cautious than I was only moments ago, and Gracie watches as his body twitches violently.

"Are you okay?" I want to hold his hands or wrap my arms around him, but it doesn't feel appropriate right now. Instead, I kneel by his side, pressing the back of my hand against his forehead to check his temperature, scanning his body for visible injuries. He's burning hot but uninjured. "August, are you okay?"

He nods his head uncertainly, but the twitching doesn't stop. He covers his mouth with his hands as he coughs, and his palms are red with blood when he pulls them away.

"He's coughing blood," Gracie whispers. "My mummy told me that people cough blood when they're dying. Is August dying?"

There's no point in trying to hide it from her anymore. "Yeah, he is."

"That's very sad." Her lips press into a pout. She's starting to look a lot older than seven.

"I know," I whisper back, wrapping an arm around her. Her head presses into my chest, and we stay like that for a few minutes, her in my arms, August's twitching slowing at my feet. When it looks like he's drifted off into a fever dream, I look back down at Gracie. "I love him very much."

"I hope I get to fall in love one day."

"I hope so too."

"But you're in love now." She falls into silent contemplation for a moment, then nods thoughtfully to herself, matter-of-factly. "Then we need to find a cure."

FOURTEEN

When I set off to find a cure, I go alone. I convince August and Gracie to head towards the gate without me, saying that I'll be able to use the map to find them again when I'm ready. However, the greater the distance between us, the less the map seems to work. The golden trail of Gracie's power fades with each step. All I can do is walk in one direction and hope that it's the right one.

The Forest has become a rainforest again, just like it was on my first day, back when I was the only one awake. I can't move without a plant brushing against me or seeing a small reptile scurrying through the undergrowth. Rain falls thickly in droplets as large as pebbles, and my clothing can only keep some of it out, but it's so warm that I almost welcome the wetness. The sweat on my skin beneath my shirt sits there and runs down my back like condensation on a windowpane. Maybe I should treat the weather like a warm shower.

I quickly lose my sense of direction. The rainforest is disorientating. It's like being dropped far out into the ocean with no sight of land, only it's not blue I'm submerged in but a thousand shades of green.

The Forest is alive with layers of sound floating through the air. A drone of unfamiliar insects hums around me. Cobwebs are stringed with delicate dewdrops glistening in the half-light. Little technicolour frogs croak under broad leaves, and one clinging to a leaf falls clammily onto my face, then into the undergrowth below. There's more life here per square foot than anywhere else on the planet and yet it's almost devoid of human life, just like that first day all over again. It feels far too familiar.

This is where I'm going to introduce some rules for walking in the Forest.

Rule one: never turn around to check behind you. You'll see nothing, but as soon as you start doing it, you won't be able to stop until your mind conjures up something that doesn't exist. Until then, an ominous feeling will follow you for the rest of your journey.

I see things in the corner of my eye, lurking in the in-between places between my state of existence and the ghosts that faded away—the flash of teeth, the curl of a claw. I wonder if I am unlike anything the Forest creatures have seen before, if this area is a wild space that has been untouched by anything other than themselves.

Rule two: you'll hear things following you, hidden in the trees all around you. Don't worry too much about it—they're just checking up on you. Similarly, if you stop walking and hear the trees calling for you, don't answer them.

I know that there are things in the Forest no one

has seen and no one will come back from unchanged. I think about Ansel's burning handprint and the blood that stains my memories, and I wonder how long is left until my luck runs out.

Rule three: don't be scared. The Forest can sense fear. Instead, just be really, really wary.

I wonder if the smoke girl is watching me from a place that I can't see, or monsters, or living corpses hanging from trees. I wonder where they go when their eyes aren't on me, if there's someone else in the distance to watch, or if they simply fade from existence when they slip out of sight. My chest tightens at the thought of them returning at any moment when I'm alone, unarmed, and off-guard.

Rule four: if you have a bad feeling about taking a certain path, you're probably right. You'll avoid whatever is waiting for you at the end of it, but all paths are bad. You can't avoid it forever. Speaking of paths, you never know what may be buried beneath the soil you're walking on. Remember that every time you take a step. Pray that whatever it is, it stays down there.

I come to a fork in the path. To the left, the rainforest continues, a muddying path snaking out of sight. To the right, I see the shadow of a boy from my memories, glimpsing the unnatural sharpness of his teeth, how his fingers bend towards the setting sun like branches. I remember how he smelled like earth, like greenery. As he grabbed my hand and led me into the trees behind his house and hung my first cigarette from his lips, a boy with forests in his eyes and wildness in his veins. Watching it back is like seeing the beginning of the end.

Now I've forgotten about him long enough to forget why I wanted to.

Maybe I've become just as wild as he was.

Rule five: make sure you remember the way back home, or at least the way you're going. The Forest will lead you astray. Your mind will lead you astray. As soon as you get lost, you're just another piece of fresh meat for the monsters.

I take the left path, the shadow fading as I turn away along with my memory of him, a blurry stranger in an old photograph. The memory twists and changes until it's not mine anymore: a boy leading me into the woods turning into my sisters and me sprawled out beneath the pine tree. Then me waking up in the Forest alone. Then the monsters advancing out of the mist, Ansel and August by my side.

And, most importantly, *rule six: you shouldn't be walking in the Forest alone.*

I know I shouldn't be afraid, but I hear something behind me. It doesn't sound human.

I run through the Forest, leaping over thin winding streams and rocks that are wet with moss. I dodge past rotting trees and snapped branches. Everything blurs into a dizzying blend of blinding green. One of my shoes slips off, and the earth soaks into my skin. I jump into a muddy brook swollen from the rain, and the Forest widens on the other side, thin layers of fallen pine needles disguising the terrain. I don't see the maze of tree-root hands reaching for me until it's too late.

When I open my eyes, I'm at home.

I fall onto my hands and knees instantly, trying to choke up stomach acid into the hydrangea bushes at the side of the path. My eyes water from the effort of it, but I can still see that what I'm actually coughing up is a weird black sludge that tastes vaguely of copper. It keeps coming until I exhaust myself and, since my eyes are already watering, it seems only a small step away from weeping. I cry on my doorstep, slumping down to the concrete face first.

It feels, for a moment, like dying all over again.

My head pounds and, even in the confusion of memories coming back in flashes, I notice a familiar haunting feeling, one I realise I've felt all along but can only put a name to as my mind is clearing, now that I know which memory I'm reliving.

Thirsty. I'm thirsty. Thirstier than I can remember. So thirsty that it drives me immediately to my feet. I'm shaky as I stand, but I steady myself against the porch and manage to stay upright. I realise it's what had driven me into the house on my dying day—an unnameable, undeniable urge.

Now that it's named, it's even more undeniable.

The need for *something* is like a living creature inside of me. I've felt something like it once before, my tongue swollen and aching, my lips cracked and bleeding as I try to lick them damp.

The house looms there as if waiting for me. I don't want to go back inside, not even a little, as I know the ending of the memory, but I must drink. I *must*. The front door is still open from when I ran out before, dying. I remember the brown envelope of paraphernalia on my bedside table, the powders that spilt across the carpet, the glass I shattered on the stairs.

But I also remember the dining area leading on from the sitting room, and the attic that was my bedroom for the few weeks we lived here before I died.

My bedroom.

With its tap.

I stop the thought again.

The thirst is nearly bending me double.

I must drink.

I walk through the front door, my throat closing

instantly as dust greets me. The floor is thick with it, muffling my uncertain footsteps, as if the house has been abandoned since I died. The air is cold and damp. For a moment, I forget my thirst.

Everything is as I left it. Scattered rays of sunlight are the only illumination as the light switches don't work in the Forest, but it's the first time I've seen pure daylight since Gracie stopped the world from turning. The room is filled with the furniture of my childhood. There are the stained red sofas—one which pulls out into a bed, the other barely bigger than an armchair—that my mother refused to replace until the baby was old enough not to mess them up anymore. Sofas that got left behind when we moved towns, left behind in the apartment where my sister died.

And there's a coffee table that was left behind and should be dozens of miles away from here in someone else's home. And the hand-painted vase the twins gifted my mother for a forgotten Christmas and accidentally broke by the New Year. And the drawing I made on the back of a restaurant menu when I learned how to hold thick crayons in my pudgy hands.

And it doesn't make any sense.

I walk up the stairs, careful not to touch the dust covering the bannister. My feet carry me to my bedroom automatically. My chest is heavy as I stumble up another set of stairs, turn the doorknob at the top, and step inside, clicking the door shut behind me.

This room is not as I left it.

The blanket fort is still set up from a rainy day a week before I died, built here after my stepfather commandeered the dining table to work. My desk chair is still adorned with a pile of clothes that are too clean for laundry, yet too dirty to put away. A collection of empty water bottles is precariously balanced across the top of the radiator. Shoes with the soles worn through are lined up against the end of my bed with expert precision, now covered thickly with dust.

But there's something different.

There's something *wrong*.

The thirst returns in full force as I think about this, so I push the thoughts away and step towards the sink that is tucked into an alcove of the room. The tap is dripping with something black. I turn the tap on full and an inky sludge pours out, flowing over the edge of the basin and into my hands and across the floor. I cup my hands, fill them with the substance, and scoop it into my mouth. It's thick like syrup and tastes like tar, but I swallow it down until my thirst eases and there's a bitterness left in my mouth. I wipe my face with the back of my hand and turn back around to examine my bedroom.

A breeze from my half-open windows sends leaves scattering across the floor. I kneel and pick one up, turning it over in my hands. It's a deep green and feels like velvet and looks like it could be from the oak tree in the neighbour's front garden. There's a slight blue tint when it catches the sunlight and my breath sticks in my throat as the realisation sinks in that even if I leave here, the Forest will still follow me home.

Maybe it's been here all along.

Behind me, my bedroom door creaks open.

When I turn around, there's no one there. I wasn't

expecting anyone to be there. But I wasn't expecting to be back in the depths of the Forest.

I spot a glow in the corner of my eye. It's water, fluorescent blue, the colour I used to shade the sky in my drawings, just like the water in the ravine. I know I shouldn't let it distract me, but I'm still so thirsty. My body throbs with exhaustion. My clothes and skin are painted with dust from my house.

I discover that the water tastes no different from tap water, if not better. I take a few gulps before stripping down to my underwear and dipping one foot into the water. It's cool against my skin, not cold. I put my other foot into the water and I slip down into the pool, the ripples closing over my head.

I hold my breath. I hold it until I can hold it no longer, and then I gulp in a breath, expecting to splutter, to choke, to drown. But I don't choke. The coolness of the water pours into my nose and my throat and fills my lungs, but that is all it does. I don't even need to hold my breath: I can breathe. The water doesn't hurt me.

I think, *This is the kind of water that you can breathe*. I think, *Perhaps there's a secret to breathing water, something simple that everyone can do if only they knew.*

The deeper I dive, the darker the water becomes, a strange type of darkness I haven't seen above the surface—clear and pure black, a night sky so rich that it's like I can see stars swirling through it. I understand they can't be real—I'm underwater, not on land looking up at the sky—but I see them straight ahead, a cluster of blue-white constellations glowing beneath me. I stop swimming for a moment, just float where I am to admire the stars, and then keep kicking downward.

Eventually, my limbs feel too heavy to swim. I don't know how deep I am or where I'm going but, even under the water, I can feel something holding my hand.

I look back up to the surface and see that I'm hanging deep below the water, deeper than what should've been possible. The starry world beneath me becomes dark as I look down. I look up once more and the world above does the same. Nothing is pulling me deeper. Nothing is forcing me up towards the surface.

I turn my head, just a little, to look at the thing

holding my hand. At first, I don't know what I'm looking at. I can't make sense of it. It's like it's made of silken sheets, burning bright, filled with a million tiny flickering flames, white butterflies in the sun. I wonder how I look to it in this place, if I'm still dark eyes and light skin and lighter hair, or if I'm also made of light.

It moves in a slow, graceful, underwater sort of movement. The current tugs at it until it moulds arms, a hand that doesn't let go of mine, a body, and an unfamiliar face. It opens its mouth and, in a foreign voice, it says, "I'm really sorry."

"What for?"

It doesn't reply. The current of this ocean pulls at my hair and my limbs like a summer breeze. I'm not drowning here or dying in my real life, and the complications of the Forest are simple and graspable and easy to understand. I am safe. I could stay here for the rest of time in this ocean beneath the pool. I could stay here forever.

"You can't," says the voice. "It will tear you apart."

I open my mouth to tell it that nothing can kill me,

not anymore, but it interrupts, "Not kill you. Tear you apart. Destroy you. Dissolve you. You won't die in here, nothing will ever die in here, but if you stay here for long enough, you will break apart until a little of you will exist everywhere."

I want to argue with it. It's wrong, it must be. I love this place, this state, this suspended feeling, and I'm never going to abandon it.

And then my head breaks the surface, and I blink and cough. I'm standing thigh-deep in the pool, and someone is standing beside me, holding my hand.

As I cough again, the water flees my nose, my throat, my lungs, everything at once. I even cough up the black sludge. I pull clean air into my chest and, in the light of the half-risen moon and the half-set sun that shines on the Forest, for one perfect moment, I feel like I'm alive.

But a woman is holding my hand.

Her beauty is intoxicating. It's difficult not to fall under the spell cast by her onyx eyes and her effortlessly captivating smile. Her skin is like the moon, waxed white, the crevices forming the shadows of her high cheekbones and arched eyebrows and defined jawline. Her hair is a mass of ebony curls pulled over one narrow shoulder. She is a princess, a queen, carved from marble. She is the person who should have the bloodstained crown on her head.

"It's nice to finally make your acquaintance, Oliver." She smiles widely, displaying her pearly teeth. She holds out her other delicate hand for me to shake but draws it back when I don't move. I'm not prepared to meet someone so obnoxiously beautiful while I'm standing in my underwear soaking wet. "My name is Carolina."

Remember August, my brain tries to interfere, and I half-heartedly pull my hand back to myself. I ignore it, fascinated by how her black dress—a corset with a long velvet skirt—outlines her narrow frame, stick thin as if she'll break if someone pushes her too hard.

"Nice to meet you, too," I reply quietly. Her beauty is something that I can't get enough of. It's like a new addiction.

Her face is level with mine as she walks around the edge of the pool. She's smiling again, barely inches away from me. She smells like an orchard. "I'm here with two choices, Oliver. I'm going to make you a deal. A promise. Your choice is whether you're going to say yes or no."

"What's your deal?"

Now, her smile is sadder. She leans forward and tilts my chin up with a slender forefinger, forcing me to look into her empty black eyes.

"There's a war coming. I want you and your friends to be on my side, Oliver. Fight for me, and you can have everything you have ever wanted."

"Everything?"

"Everything."

"Even a cure for August?"

She sighs, her smile faltering for a second as her hand drops to her side. "The Forest does not possess the power to control anything that exists outside of its boundaries. August's living body is the thing that is hurting him."

"There isn't a cure."

"Not in this world."

I sink back into the water, only my head above the surface. "I'm sorry, but I can't join you. *We* can't join you. We're going to be home before a war starts. We already have a way home."

The words slip out of my mouth before I can stop them. I don't trust Carolina and, if she knows about our way home, she'll know that she'll have to make the journey harder for me for turning down her offer.

She's standing again, rearranging her silk cloak around her shoulders, fussing with an elaborate silver brooch that clasps the material together at her throat. "Is that so?"

I nod, watching as her eyes fill with venom.

"So be it."

I wake abruptly with my head below the surface of the pool and a mouth full of glowing water. I dreamt I was awake, and Carolina came to me in my sleep.

There's no sign of her presence besides a tweed knapsack that's hidden beneath the pile of my dusty clothes and one remaining shoe. It's full of clean clothes, and I'm relieved that they fit me perfectly. I dress in charcoal-coloured breeches tucked into strong leather boots, a white tunic, and a black wool jerkin. There's a scabbard attached to a belt that I tie around my waist, even though it doesn't hold a blade.

Satisfied with my outfit change, I set off into the Forest, abandoning my search for a cure and choosing to look for Ansel instead.

FIFTEEN

I'm being followed. Not by people or monsters this time, no. I'm being followed by wolves.

I turn and see one in the distance, sniffing the ground, tracking something. Tracking *me*. I take off barrelling through the trees only to find a stone wall that blocks my way, stretching as far as I can see in both directions. Judging the height of it, I try to find handholds to climb it, but I slide back down and land in a heap on the ground.

A throaty growl shoots icicles into my blood.

The wolves line up, pinning me between them and the wall, the leader in front and four others behind.

213

It's easier for me to see their unnaturally sparkling eyes up close, as if they're lit from within by some kind of wicked magic. Their fur is patchy; scraps of metal have replaced it where it's missing.

The leader's growl grows in intensity. It takes a step forward. I fling myself at the wall again, digging with my fingers, trying to find a handhold. My boots slide against the stones. A hand almost reaches the top, but I can't find a grip with my feet.

With a snarl, the lead wolf leaps forward, its teeth catching hold of my breeches, trying to drag me down. I yelp as the fabric rips across my calf, setting me free, and I frantically claw my way higher up the hall, scraping my palms in desperation.

Then a hand reaches over the wall, grabs my collar, and hauls me over.

"Watch yourself next time." The voice is raspy like an old man after a lifetime of smoking and alcohol abuse, but there are no adults in this Forest. The voice belongs to a child, maybe a few years younger than me, trying to sound older than he is. "You shouldn't be walking outside of the walls on your own."

I nod without looking for too long at my saviour, then run in the opposite direction towards a familiar castle.

No one tries to stop me as I walk inside. No one even looks my way, probably thinking that I'm one of them. I walk down the centre of the sprawling corridors, and everyone steps out of my way to avoid bumping into me. It's like I'm trying to be seen.

Coming back here so soon is accompanied by a feeling of dread, and the image of Catherine's lifeless body appears each time I blink. The deeper I get into the castle, the more the scent of her blood overwhelms my senses. And the burning red welts across her throat. And the sound of her sobbing beneath the gag.

Then I spot a girl. A living one.

She's made of metal.

Partially, at least. Metal flows over the flesh on the left side of her body as if she's been dipped in brass. She scratches at the meeting point between the metal and her skin. It's flaming red, as if she's been scratching for hours.

I follow the girl from what feels like a safe distance. She takes a left near the end of the main corridor, a right off that one, and goes down a secluded staircase. I follow her into a room with one wall lined with beds like a hospital wing. All the beds are empty except one; a blonde girl rests in the one furthest from the door. A boy stands in the room's corner, sword leaning against the wall behind him, knife at his waist.

"How is she?" the brass girl asks the boy, still scratching at her arm. Her gaze doesn't leave the blonde.

The boy steps into the light. A flickering lantern casts dancing shadows across his face, exaggerating his cheekbones and pushing his eyes deeper into their sockets. It makes him look older, more haunted. "They put the cure on her just like they did for you. It didn't work. She's still resting." He rubs his face with the back of his hand. "It was a struggle to get her to calm down."

A silence of unspoken secrets fills the room. The girl looks at the boy, then the floor, then at the girl on the bed. Her face softens when she looks at her. "I hope she's okay," she murmurs. She scratches at her arm once more, then moves towards the girl.

As she grows closer, the soft flesh on the blonde's hands melts away, the creamy skin turning brown as aged copper appears in its place.

"Hazel!" the boy cries, fumbling for his knife. "Look out!"

The moment he calls out the warning, the blonde's entire body becomes solid metal from her hair to her battered trainers. It's as if she's been coated in copper, every fine detail of her features preserved. Not an automaton, but a moving statue. A soldier.

"What have they done to me?" it screams, lunging forward and tightening its hands around the brass girl's—Hazel's—neck. "What have you done to me?"

If it had been a regular teenage girl, Hazel could have easily escaped, but this version has her in a death grip and continues to tighten it the more she struggles. The creature doesn't seem to care that they share the same metal. The human part of it sees a friend. The metal part of it sees an enemy that must be destroyed.

The boy dives towards Hazel, hacking at the

creature with his knife, but it does no good.

"A sword, get a sword! Get it!" Hazel chokes out, wheezing as her captor tightens its grip further, lifting so her boots are barely brushing the floor. Her face, at least the skin that remains, is a dusky purple as she fights for breath. Kicking out, she tries to break the grip.

The metal girl laughs at her feeble effort.

Behind them, the boy hefts the sword and nearly drops it. It looks heavier than he is. The second time, he puts his back into it and gets the blade into the air, letting gravity do its worst on the outstretched arms. The sword bounces off the metal, doing it no harm, so he tries again. This time, when his blow strikes the creature, it breaks its grip and releases a horrifying, inhuman screech.

I'm about to yell, but someone clamps a silvery hand down over my mouth.

Porcelain's grip tightens when I start to struggle. "What are you doing back here?" she demands, the scars on her hands shimmering with each movement in the lamplight. I imagine her eyes are glimmering the same way. "Lilac gave you the chance to leave freely once before. She will not be that generous again."

Should I be afraid of the child in a shiny hat? I shrug Porcelain's hands off me, then try to summarise the situation as well as I can. "August's body is dying. We've found the way home. I'd like it if August survived until we can get him home." Then, after a moment of thought, "I think Ansel is here, too."

I turn around to face Porcelain. She rolls her eyes. They're golden brown and flecked with iron. "Ansel has arrived. Lilac has requested for him to join her court, but he is showing resistance. She knows who he is and his connection to your Gracie, and he could become a valuable player in the war, although not an important one."

My head swarms with questions, but I don't know which one will give me the answer I need the most. "What's the court?" I ask to begin with.

She leads me out of the room and back up the stairs as she answers, "A King or Queen often has a group of companions to advise them about decisions that will affect their kingdom. The current court is formed by some of the earliest inhabitants of the Forest who are yet to move on. Lilac has earned the crown, so she needs a court to stop her from damaging this world further."

"Are you part of the court?"

"I am. But many of us do not wish to be and would prefer the choice to return home, just like you. Most of the army that Lilac is building has no choice but to follow her every command. Some of us are free from her control and plan to turn against her when the time is right. I dislike being less powerful than a child tyrant." She cracks the door and peers out into the corridor. "Because of this, I have chosen to help you."

If the sun still sets in the west, I work out that Porcelain guides me to the eastern turret of the castle and up the stairs, then pushes me into a dark room and closes the door behind me. She mutters something about getting answers from the other side.

At first, the darkness of the room deceives me, or

my eyes are still confused and dazzled by the glare of the light outside. For a minute or two, I can make out nothing besides dark lumps of furniture covered in sheets, an exposed chest of drawers by the wall, and a patch of white paint marking something on the floor.

"I see you." A voice echoes through the darkness.

I bite back a shout at the sudden sound before someone—*something*—hears. But the thing already sees me, and the irregular tune of my breathing and the racing thud of my heart is too loud to stay hidden any longer.

"Do you see me?"

I turn around.

A man stands a few paces away from me. His body is covered in a patchwork burlap cloak, and his face is masked with a shadow cast by a battered top hat. When he walks towards me, his movements are mechanic, sometimes smooth as a blade across the ice but broken by the occasional jerk and shudder. That's when I realise he isn't a man: he is a toy.

"I see you," I whisper when he is within touching

distance, afraid to be any louder.

I see how one half of his face is constructed from cream cotton stretched over painted plastic instead of flesh and muscle. I see how his hair is brightly coloured wool and yarn, appealing to childlike eyes. I see how, when he pulls back his cloak, his body is entirely made of a metal skeletal structure.

"You don't belong here," he says, a cog whirring around where his heart should be, making the sound of an elderly man wheezing. "This is not your home."

I nod, although I'm not sure how well he can see me. "I know. It's different here from where I'm supposed to be. I don't know how I got here, but I know there's a way home."

The Toyman's only response is to lean on a metal cane he pulls out from beneath his cloak, his one real and one fake eye scanning me from head to toe. I wonder how much my appearance has changed since I've been here. I wonder if I still look like myself.

"Tell me about your...home."

That's what I do. I tell him about Earth, a summary

of all the different continents and climates and cultures, before narrowing it down to just my town in the middle of nowhere. I describe my house and my siblings and the different walks I used to take to school. I explain to him about my life before he tells me about his.

"I am a...toy."

"Who made you like this?" I ask.

"Lilac Bonneville." He breathes slowly, as if the answer pains him. "We are in a world that runs on imagination, and hers is the strongest of all."

The image of the tiny girl in a bloodstained crown fills my vision. I remember the army of mechanical soldiers, and Porcelain hinting that this world won't exist for much longer. "If she made you, what else has she made?"

"She made two keys and hid them both. Together, they unlock a gate that will take you back to the place you love the most."

My eyes widen. "Where are the keys? How can I find them?"

He hesitates as if he doesn't want to tell me. The cog in his chest whirrs faster. "One key is stolen from who holds the crown. One key is held when the crown has been stolen. That is all I can tell you. That is all I have been allowed to tell others like you."

I'm suddenly reminded of a pair of empty black eyes. "Do you know about a woman named Carolina? She visited me. She said something about a war coming."

He nods. The movement makes his neck groan from the rust.

He tells me his story. Before Lilac came to the Forest and started to understand her abilities, Carolina was the Queen. She was like the Queen of Hearts, stealing the heart of anyone who she deemed worthy, turning them into a heartless soldier she could manipulate into fighting for her way back home. She spent too long building her army that hundreds of years passed in the Otherworld, time taking her body with it. Even if she found a way through the gate, she wouldn't be able to leave.

It's here that I realise that the mechanical soldiers in the cave didn't belong to Lilac.

"Carolina has nothing left to return to, so she has started a new life here," the Toyman says, his voice barely audible over his whirring heart. It sounds like he's panicking. "She has an army to use now, even if many are now loyal to the crown. She wants power over anyone who could help her out of the Forest. She wants the crown back."

Then he steps back and fades into the shadows. The room I'm standing in becomes empty once more.

I set off to continue my search for Ansel and to find two hidden keys.

Porcelain is waiting for me outside of the room.

"What was in there?" she asks eagerly, the silver flecks in her eyes glinting with childlike curiosity. The colours match the circlet that she wears on her head, half-covered by her dark hair.

"You sent me into a room without knowing what was in there?"

Her eyes are still flickering like candlelight. "Lilac

goes in there whenever she needs answers that I cannot provide for her. I hear her talking through the door. Tell me, what was in there?"

I describe the Toyman to her, every detail from what he said about Carolina's army to the colours of yarn I could see in his hair. She falls silent as I mimic the sound of the whirring cog that replaces his heartbeat. Her brow crinkles when I tell her about the clue for finding the keys.

"One key is stolen from who holds the crown. That must mean Lilac has a hidden key." I state the obvious, but Porcelain nods along, hair bouncing on her shoulders.

She picks up the skirt of her dress and begins walking down the stairs, quickly rounding a corner out of my sight. She talks as she walks. "It could be hidden on her person. But a key that is held when the crown has been stolen? I do not know what that could mean."

"It doesn't matter. We can work out where to find the first key."

SIXTEEN
AUGUST

I kneel at the edge of a river, scrubbing my nails into my palms until the skin burns raw. Another cough racks through my body that spatters the water with red. It doesn't seem as if I'll ever be able to get the blood off my hands, and they don't feel clean even after I've scrubbed off a layer of skin. It looks like the chipped ruby nail polish that once stained my stepmother's fingertips. I scrub harder.

In my daydream, it's a few weeks after I blew out fourteen candles on my birthday cake and hoped that the memories of conversion therapy would disappear along with the flames.

It's mid-October, and I'm sitting in an armchair that belongs to my mother's mother. I'm still not sure if she found me or if I found her, but she invited me to her bungalow and spread my mother's childhood photo albums across the carpet, cooing about how alike we look if you ignore the eyes. She shows me an old jewellery box and tells me to take whatever I want. It belongs to me, after all. I take a handmade ring and wear it on a long piece of yarn beneath my t-shirt every single day. After that, I never see my mother's mother again.

It's late November, and my best friend is sitting on the curb outside my house, leaning against a suitcase with their ripped denim jacket slung over one shoulder. Their father and his new girlfriend couldn't stand having a child who wouldn't eat—not even for their birthday meal—so they kicked them out.

I haven't seen my best friend since before I was sent away, and don't know how to act around them anymore, just that I should pretend that nothing is wrong. Because nothing is wrong with me anymore, right? My best friend doesn't know what's changed, only that I had been away for a few months after the rumours and came back different, but they're happy that we can still sneak out late to lie in the fields.

My best friend's suitcase lives on my bedroom floor for the next few days as we curl up in my twin-sized bed and sleep in half the day and watch reruns of reality shows, their hand lingering for too long on the small of my back. They ask me to let them live with me for a while, not as long as last time, they hope. I agree because we're best friends, aren't we?

They officially move into my house four days after they arrive on the curb, and the two of us walk to school together each morning, hands brushing with each step, and walk home together every evening, and become so in tune with one another that we can have an entire conversation with only a glance. 'A while' becomes a lot longer, and they celebrate their fifteenth birthday at my house in the following late November, holding their breath to make a wish before they blow out the candles.

I pretend not to notice the colours that flicker across my vision along with the flames.

SEVENTEEN

The first place we decide to search is Lilac's bedroom.

The room is sparsely furnished, but it's full of more warmth than I've seen since I arrived in the Forest. On the back wall, there's a framed painting of a tree with every colour of autumn leaf imaginable and a few more. From the other three walls, faces smile back in black and white photographs of Lilac and people who I assume to be her mother, her father, and a sister. There's a single bed with plain sheets and large windows curtained by squares of starched white cotton.

"Search wherever you can, but leave no trace."

I can already tell that we won't find the key here, but I look around anyway, even sliding under the bed to search the underside of the mattress. It's dark under here, but it's a nice darkness, one that reminds me of the blanket forts of my childhood where we'd turn off all the lights in the apartment and tell stories by torchlight and pretend that we were camping outside. Rowan would help me build the fort, dragging around the furniture and pushing it together. I would drape the structure in blankets and bedsheets and cover the floor with sofa cushions.

A lump forms in my throat as I linger on the memory. I long for the home that I've lost. It fills me with determination to find the keys, find a way to keep August alive, and then find the way home.

"It is not here," Porcelain concludes after a few minutes of searching. She looks over at me, and I pretend that I'm busy, not just lying on the floor. "We will search somewhere else. Come with me."

I follow her through the castle again, down a set

of stairs, up another, round a few corners, ducking into darkened doorways and empty rooms whenever someone comes our way.

The next room is blue with beautiful murals on the walls, hand-painted by someone who knew what they were doing. The scene shows a night sky filled with swirling clouds, stars ablaze with their own luminescence, and a bright gibbous moon. Below the rolling hills of the horizon lies a small town with a tall steeple of a church reigning over the smaller buildings. To the left of the painting, there is a massive dark structure that I can't identify, magnificent when compared to the scale of the other objects.

Porcelain catches me staring and hurriedly tugs a heavy velvet drape across the mural. This must be her room, and that painting must be too personal for anyone but her to lay their eyes on.

"We are going to search the dungeons as soon as I find the key," she informs me, rummaging through a drawer. "I hope that you are not afraid of the dark."

The dungeons lay at the bottom of a series of what feels like never-ending staircases, the light fading as we descend each level. Porcelain carries a candle, but it doesn't make much of a difference. I don't notice when we arrive; the darkness doesn't differ between the staircases and the dungeon. Porcelain drags me towards a specific cell and unlocks the barred door.

Cramped, dim, and cave-like, a spindly wooden bed frame has been cut shorter to fit into the space, and a narrow strip of carpet greying with decades of filth is placed to the left side. To the right, there is an inch-wide window layered in ageing mould and dust that looks out on the dirt beneath the castle. Drawers are overflowing with moth-eaten, child-sized clothes and bedding thriving with maggots and grime.

"This is pleasant," I say, choking on the dust in the air. "I've never been to a dungeon with a carpet before. Look, there's even a change of clothes."

Porcelain's glare is enough to shut me up. "Look for the key."

I look through the doorway and see an identical cell across the corridor. There's a young boy—maybe eleven or twelve—locked inside, leaning against the bars, lazily clicking his fingers together. A flurry of amber sparks flies between his fingertips. He is painfully thin, as if he's been starved, but his eyes are nothing more than bored. It's like he's biding his time.

Around his throat is a band of copper. It ripples across the surrounding skin, and I remember why it looks so familiar: I saw it happen on Lilac's arm. When he notices me watching, he tugs at the skin as if it hurts, but his expression remains unreadable.

I look away and step back into the cell. I'm not tempted to rummage through the dirt and bugs that live within it. "What do the keys even look like?"

Porcelain sees my hesitation to search and crosses the room in three quick steps, tugging out a drawer entirely and dumping the contents on the ground. There isn't a key hidden inside. "They are skeleton keys made from dark metal. By now, they will be rusty. I think—" A loud crash from somewhere above us cut her off. Her eyes widen in alarm. "Something is wrong. Something is very, very wrong."

"I guess I should follow you?"

She glares at me again. I don't blame her. "Yes. You should."

The occupants of the castle are gathered outside in the courtyard. I see a few familiar faces, but none of them are Ansel. A dozen teenagers dressed in simple white clothes stand in the centre of the courtyard. Lilac stands in front of them, her crown reflecting the half-light, but nothing she says is changing their distressed expressions. With each second, she becomes angrier. The ground around her shakes.

"What is going on?" Porcelain demands, grabbing the nearest person's sleeve and pulling them so they're face to face. Her eyes are less like metal and more like stone.

"Lilac called everyone together. The court is unsettled. Something's wrong."

She sighs in frustration. "I already know that something is wrong. What is the problem?"

"There's a large group of newcomers in the Forest. They met up with some other people that we haven't found yet. All of them have found a gate, but they can't use it yet. They're working on...alternate methods to leave. Some of our people have left the castle to join them. Half of the court is missing."

"They cannot do that! That would be suici—"

A column of dirt surges upwards from where Lilac is standing. Her powers transform her into a figure with thick arms and chubby legs. The limbs elongate as she rises in height, first ten, then twenty feet above the courtyard. The round, pudgy face sits above a massive neck and chest. It's unmistakably female and completely nude.

I wince. "I think I'm now scarred for life. What is that thing?"

Porcelain shakes her head in disgust but it doesn't quite mask the look of amazement in her eyes. She's impressed by the thing that Lilac has become. "That is what Lilac was working on in her free time over the past few weeks, since the last time you were within our walls. I was not expecting her to succeed so quickly."

"I've been gone for weeks? Wait, that doesn't matter. How is becoming a giant monster a success?"

Lilac bellows and stomps at the ground, sending some of her remaining court members flying. One flails through the air and is thrown against a tree. I hear their neck snap, then they stop moving. Blood pools beneath their body. With another bellow, the bloodstained crown falls from Lilac's head and crashes onto the ground.

Porcelain stares as it rolls in circles. Then she looks up at Lilac, stomping around as she adjusts to her new form. "She could not find a warrior, so she became one."

"What do we do now?" I ask. The ground shakes more violently, and it's a struggle to stay on my feet. "Do we kill her? Is this your cue to turn against the crown?"

"No, of course not! She is just a child. We must

restrain her and reason with her until she changes back if she still can."

I pretend not to hear the last four words of the sentence.

Lilac stops stomping. She reaches out a hand and wiggles her fingers until the ground bursts open. Some familiar monsters crawl out of the hole.

The first few move slowly, slime dripping from their skin, oozing puddles of a sickly white substance onto the ground. The stone slabs of the courtyard instantly dissolve and the substance burns into the dirt beneath.

The next few monsters are a mass of tangled limbs plated with paralysing goo seeping from black pores. They click their teeth together and look around with one eye. They're as tall as a bus, but still nowhere near as tall as Lilac. As she wiggles her fingers to summon more of her creations, they emit a series of squeaks and clicks.

The final few appear as a cluster of jelly-like eggs at first, vibrating as they assess the beginnings of the battle and change their shape. They turn metallic green and let out coloured sparks as they crush themselves together and form mightier monsters as tall and as wide as a truck.

"Do we kill these?" I ask Porcelain, gesturing to the swarm of monsters that continues to grow. "Or should we let them kill us?"

"Now? We do nothing," Porcelain whispers. She grabs my wrist and pulls me to the edge of the courtyard, hiding in the shadows of the castle walls. "She would not do all this just to find some people who are trying to leave the Forest. She would send soldiers after them. This is about something else, something bigger."

That's when I spot someone stepping into the courtyard, covered in a green cloak. Tufts of black hair stick out from the edge of the hood.

"Oh, this is much worse than I thought," Porcelain mutters. "Much, much worse."

"What's going on?" I ask.

The living members of the court are walking away from Lilac, but the cloaked figure remains. They reach up to their throat, fumble at the cloak clasp, and let it drop to the ground. It reveals a skinny teenage boy with round cheeks smeared with dirt. One side of his body is blistering from a burning handprint. At his waist swings a sword that used to belong to me.

"There is your Ansel," Porcelain informs me. "He must have challenged Lilac for the crown."

EIGHTEEN

As soon as Ansel reaches the first of the monsters, I know that this is a fight that won't last for more than a second. Maybe two, if he's lucky.

"I wouldn't say it's much of a challenge," I say, watching as Porcelain paces frantically, hands knotted in her hair. "Lilac is a huge monster and has an army of monsters that she can summon whenever she needs them. She has powers and can bend the Forest to do whatever she wants. Ansel has…Well, Ansel has nothing. He has a burn and probably a black eye and a broken nose. He's just Ansel."

"I am aware of that," she mutters.

I scan the courtyard again, watching Ansel as he pulls his sword free, fumbles, and then drops it to the ground. Most of the castle's inhabitants are standing on the sidelines, but some take a tentative step forward. They join Ansel's side. The fight is still unfair.

Then I catch a glimpse of a familiar blue raincoat in the lower branches of a distant tree. Gracie holds out her hand, squeezes it into a fist, and watches as the nearest monster crumbles into a pile of dust. The corner of the map peeks out from the end of a sleeve, and I wonder how she managed to get it back. Her bright eyes catch mine, and she smiles and waves as if I'm seeing her from across a street rather than what is about to become a battleground.

Gracie turns away to continue crushing monsters from her safe spot. My heart sinks a little when I don't spot August by her side, so I can only hope that he's somewhere safe, somewhere still alive.

"What do you think you should do?" Porcelain asks me, although the tone of her voice makes it sound as if the answer is obvious. "You can turn away and keep searching for keys and cures for your lover, or you can stay here and fight by the side of the boy who left you. The boy who wants to become a King. It is your decision."

The answer is obvious. It should be. I just don't choose it. "I'm going to fight with Ansel. Gracie adores him, and she will not let us go home without him."

Porcelain nods, her brow furrowing. "If that is what you wish, I will fight with you."

"Thanks."

"You are welcome."

With that, Porcelain thrusts a sword into my hands, removes her bow from her shoulder, and starts running. I try to sprint after her but she's a lot quicker than me, as if she's been training for battle her entire afterlife. She fires arrows and kills monsters as she runs. I struggle to carry the sword and hold it awkwardly between both hands, not knowing how to make it feel natural, let alone swing it and hit a target.

"What exactly are we doing?" I shout to Porcelain.

She nods in Lilac's direction. "We must immobilise her. Find a blind spot by her feet." She loads her bow with three arrows and each finds a target. "The Achilles tendon is where you should aim. Do not lose your weapon. Do not get stepped on."

"This would be an appropriate time to tell you I failed biology in school," I say just before she disappears into the fight.

She rolls her eyes. "The back of the heel."

"Got it."

She rolls her eyes again, turns on her heel, and is consumed by a crowd of people, some running away from the fight, some running towards it. There's nothing else for me to do besides tighten my grip on the sword and start running straight towards Lilac.

By now, she has fully adjusted to her new form, gleefully crushing anyone who gets too close beneath her feet, picking up her own soldiers who don't move fast enough in a giant fist and hurling them into the trees. There's nothing left that reminds me of the young girl I saw on the throne, not even the bloodstained crown.

It makes me feel slightly better about needing to hurt her.

There's already a soldier at Lilac's feet, barely older than me. Her swordplay is flashy but a waste of time, even if she manages to viciously slice Lilac's skin without being stomped on. Lilac isn't doing too well—bad eye-foot coordination—and she bellows in frustration every time she misses. It only makes my eardrums ache and the ground quiver.

"You're big and noisy. We've got that," I mutter.

In a lunatic show of courage, a white-clad soldier races up and jumps, jamming his sword into Lilac's leg. It has little effect other than making her bellow even louder. He barely manages to scurry away when a huge hand tries to grab him. He cries out as Lilac swats at him, sending him tumbling across the courtyard. My heart races until I see him crawl back onto his feet. Still, he's moving too slowly, and if I don't do something...

While Lilac is distracted, I close the distance between us, my sword swinging uncomfortably by my side. I weigh it in my right hand, slashing delicately with apprehension. I'm satisfied with the weapon; it's too late for me to learn how to use it, but I may not have to use it more than once.

I raise the sword, aim between the base of Lilac's calf and the top of her heel, and thrust the blade forward as hard as I can. She roars and lifts her foot in the air, my sword hanging out of her thick skin. She pulls it out—the blade the size of a toothpick between her fingers—and throws it at the ground. I watch as it clatters in front of me. The blade is bent beyond use. I'll have to find something else that can hurt her.

A flicker of metal in the half-light catches my eye. There's a wristwatch half-buried beneath a broken courtyard tile, not a colourful plastic one, but an expensive one where the gold glints casually in the fading sunlight. It's broken: the hands don't turn, and the face has been crushed from the impact. It looks different from when I last saw it wrapped around Lilac's wrist.

I may not be able to hurt her physically, but I have the one thing that can wound her emotionally.

I don't have the chance to.

There's a glint of metal as someone hurls a shield across the courtyard. It connects with my temple before I can duck, and my vision flickers to black once more.

I stand in the centre of a vast darkness. There's a dull spotlight on me. I glance down at my hands and body and find myself dressed in white clothes that I don't recognise. I'm barefoot, and the soles of my feet are burning hot. The hair on the back of my neck stands up as I feel eyes in the darkness.

The empty wasteland horrifies me. My eyes can't penetrate the darkness, no matter which way I turn. It's the complete absence of light except for the circle around me. The darkness weighs heavily on my shoulders, brooding and rotating around me. The sheer depth of my aloneness elevates my fear to a level I've never known.

I hear muffled voices spilling out to my left side.

Mocking laughter from the right. Waves of rejection and hatred sweep through me from behind. I try to run from it all, but I slam into an invisible barrier, restricted to the circle of the spotlight.

An unholy voice speaks from below me. "Wait your turn. We will be with you sooner than you want."

The laughter to the right intensifies and presses in, so I wait.

Seconds drag into minutes. Minutes melt into what feels like hours. I count time, tracking each second and minute until I do reach an hour. That's when I decide to speak. "Am I dead? Like, properly this time?"

The laughter stops. I've never heard silence quite this loud.

"You will not die yet," the voice says, and I've never been angrier at nothingness. I want to scream, so I do.

In the intense silence, I somehow scream with my whole body. My eyes wide with horror, mouth rigid and open, chalky face gaunt and immobile, fists clenched with whitened knuckles and nails drawing blood from the palms of my hands. I almost feel alive.

Then I go quiet, just panting. The spotlight on me fades into darkness.

Darkness is a strange substance. It doesn't fall under the laws of physics as it's a sort of mystical material, only able to change states by the user. As a solid, it's almost completely black aside from a tiny spot of red at the centre like a candle in the dark, a pinprick of blood in your vision. As a liquid, it's thick and sticky, has a pungent smell of ink, and can act like quicksand to suffocate people. As a gas, it's able to pass through solid material with ease and eat away like acid.

And the darkness is eating away at me.

As the final breaths of air drain out of my lungs, I wonder if there's any point in continuing to breathe.

I wake up just in time to avoid being crushed by the body of a falling soldier. Porcelain sees me rolling across the ground and sprints towards me, firing multiple arrows from her bow at once. From the sound of the monster's screams, I assume she hasn't missed a target yet.

"Glad to see you alive," she says blankly, not letting me be a distraction to her.

Pulling myself back to my feet is painstaking: my legs are numb, and my left arm is twisted at an unnatural angle. It doesn't hurt. Lilac's watch remains in my wounded fist. I take a cautious step forward, and my feet slip against the fresh blood on the ground. Looking down, I sigh. I've lost one of my boots.

"How is she still alive?" I groan, seeing that Lilac is stomping around, bellowing at everything that moves. Porcelain shoves me back to the ground, shooting an arrow at a monster behind me. The ash from the disintegrated body sticks to the blood on my feet. I groan again before pocketing the watch, double-checking my surroundings for imminent threats.

"The Queen can only die at the hands of a sacrifice."

"It's starting to sound like you're making things up on the spot." I sigh, taking a few steps to see how well my legs will hold my weight. My arm throbs, but I can ignore it for a few moments longer. "Well, no one has tried to kill me for a minute or two."

I'm about to run across the courtyard when someone grabs hold of my uninjured arm.

"Don't you dare."

There's a smile on my face before I even turn around, but I'm not prepared for what I see.

August's bruises have returned worse than ever. It's difficult to find a patch of skin that is still the untouched colour. There's a trail of blood coming out of the corner of his mouth and another from his nose. His exposed arms are covered by vicious scratches.

"Are you okay?" I ask, even though the answer is clear.

He tries to smile, but the effort makes him wince. It isn't reassuring that he can't hide the pain from his injuries anymore. "I'll survive, but you won't if you go out there."

"Did you hear what Porcelain said? Lilac can only be stopped if there's a sacrifice. If it's not me, it'll be Ansel as he fights for the crown."

"I heard." He nods slowly, almost sadly. "Neither of you is going to be the sacrifice, not if I can help it."

"If I don't, who will?"

Then I remember who August came here with.

"August, where's Gracie?"

He doesn't have the chance to answer.

Something explodes.

A fist of orange flame punches its way out of the ground.

Tiles and slabs shatter, sending pieces of stone showering down in a deadly rainfall.

The force of the explosion lifts us into the air and throws us across the courtyard.

I lay in agony and semi-blindness amid chaos. All around me, bodies drop to the ground one by one. I lay there until I recover consciousness, trying to control my breathing and work out if any of my injuries are life-threatening.

At first, I think I've gone deaf. The ringing of swords has died away, and the shouting of slaughter is hushed. Silence lies on what remains of the red-stained courtyard. Garish scarlet blooms over the frosted grey of the stone.

Then I realise the battlefield is quiet because it's now a graveyard of the unburied. Discarded weapons lay among the corpses rather than flowers. The half-set sun still shines, the wind still blows, and the birds still screech in harmony, but there are families who will wake up in the Otherworld and receive the news that their child has died. These children who would've once ridden bikes in the street and fallen asleep to bedtime stories are now nothing more than memories and meat for the Forest creatures. Their eyes are as immobile as their limbs.

Then I hear quiet footsteps skip over the rubble. I twist my head around, cheek scraping against broken shards of stone.

Gracie is standing in the centre of the courtyard, the bodies of a hundred fallen children and teenagers surrounding her, covered in dust from the monster's remains. She's staring straight up at Lilac, her hand outstretched. There's a ghost of a smile on her face.

I try to stand, try to get onto my feet so I can run over and keep her safe one last time, but August throws an arm over me and pins me to the ground.

Porcelain kneels beside us. Her bow is drawn, but I don't think she'll aim it at me if I try to run. "Do not interfere. This is what she has to do."

"Why has it got to be her?" Angry tears form in my eyes, and they burn as they drip down my face. "Why can't it be anyone else? Why isn't it Ansel?"

Porcelain sighs sadly, and I wonder how many sacrifices she's seen before, how many monarchs she's lived through. "It is what all children like her have to do."

I don't want to watch Gracie's final moments, but I force myself to. There's nothing more painful than watching the death of a child who was never destined to survive.

NINETEEN

There are two bodies on the ground, both belonging to children, laying side by side. They don't look anything alike, but they are opposite sides of the same cursed coin.

Gracie lies on the left. Her raincoat is torn, showing a sunflower yellow blouse beneath, although it is now dulled with dirt. The map survived the battle and is clutched in her tiny fist. She's scratched her own additions into the fabric, noting constellations and caves and castles. Her hazel eyes stare blankly into the sky. August presses his thumbs against her eyelids and closes her eyes for the last time. One of his tears drips onto her cheek.

"Sleep tight, little warrior," I murmur, tucking the map back into her coat. "Find your way back home for me."

Lilac lies on the right. Her white-blonde curls are tangled so they look like dandelion fluff. The absence of the crown has left a line burned across her forehead, forever branding her a Queen of the Forest. Her eyes are the same deep blue as the jewels she once wore on her head, and I'm the one who leans forward to close them. Her face is now free from the scowl that almost became familiar. I kneel by her side, pull her limp arm onto my lap, and put the broken watch back on her wrist. Porcelain takes the crown from where it rests beside Lilac's head and smoothes her hair until it's flat.

"They're just children," August whispers. His voice cracks and his crying becomes hysterical, the desperate sobs only interrupted by his need to breathe.

My eyes also fill with tears, but I can't bring myself to let them fall. To be so close to so much pain changes a person, even temporarily. My own pain rises a little closer to the surface, and I can't walk away or I'll get a kick of guilt as punishment.

Porcelain doesn't seem to feel the same emotions. In fact, she doesn't seem to have any emotions, as if she's one of Carolina's metal soldiers.

"This does not belong to her anymore," she says, ignoring how August has sunk to his knees and buried his face in his hands. She stands and holds the crown in one hand, fumbling inside it with the other. She grips something and pulls. "I believe we have found part of what we were looking for."

She holds out her hands towards me. In one, she still holds the crown, flakes of rust and dried blood settling in her palm. In the other, she holds a key. It's a skeleton key, about the length of my hand, from the tip of my middle finger to my wrist. It's made from dark metal, and it's thick with rust.

Then I suddenly realise what the key is.

"One key is stolen from who holds the crown." The Toyman's words come back to me so vividly that I can hear his wheezing and the whirring of his heart in my mind. "And one key is held when the crown has been stolen. So, where is the other key?"

Porcelain tucks the key into the folds of her dress and looks down at the crown. Her fingers trace across the patterns moulded into the metal. "The crown being stolen suggests physically stealing it from the leader of the Forest—which is impossible—or it can suggest an uprising. We have had both, but this key was hidden with Lilac. I am not sure which part of the riddle this key represents."

"Can we just hope that this is the hidden key?" August says. His face reddens as he holds back a cough. I pretend not to notice and resist the urge to fuss over him.

"We might have to. We started looking and couldn't find anything." I turn to Porcelain. "How can we know for certain that the crown is stolen?"

She pauses for a second as she thinks, winding a dark curl around her finger. She pulls it straight before it springs back into place. "We need to have a crowning ceremony. If a new monarch is crowned, then it will be well and truly stolen."

"How do we do that? How soon?"

"We will need an appropriate person to take Lilac's place and participate in the ceremony." Porcelain walks across the courtyard. I think she's taking note of who died and who could still be alive. "Her court has disbanded as well as most of her army. Rebel soldiers will need someone to guide them out of the Forest but that was expected of you before as you are the ones who hold a map and knowledge of a gate."

"Then it would make sense if one of us took the crown," August murmurs. He wipes his nose with the back of his hand, smearing blood across the lower half of his face. The Forest is no longer doing anything to heal him. It isn't doing anything to heal me, either: Porcelain made a splint for my injured arm from two of her arrows and a spare bowstring. I don't want to believe that one of us could die soon.

The three of us stand in silence as we contemplate the decision.

As I think, my eyes drift to the sky. To the west, the

horizon is aglow with the last amber embers of the sun, trapped in the perpetual half-light as they attempt to push themselves below the treeline. The clouds are dyed pomegranate red. To the east, the bulk of the castle blocks how twilight beckons the constellations forming in the lower part of the sky.

"Before you make this choice, I will tell you about the powers of the crown." Porcelain returns to us, done with assessing the dead. "The crown holds a power that most of us do not know the extent of. If you wear it, you cannot take it off. It will heal you to full health, but I have been told that there are severe consequences of using the power."

I'm not the one who needs healing, but I don't want to risk harming August further if we're close to finding our way home.

"You said that most people don't know what the crown can do," I repeat. "That must mean that there's at least one person out there who does. Is it the Toyman?"

Porcelain shakes her head. "No. He will not exist for much longer now that Lilac is dead. He was something she pulled out of her imagination. There is someone who existed here before Lilac, before any of the current inhabitants of the Forest, who will understand the true powers of the crown."

"Do you have to pay the consequences instantly, or can we try the crown on for size and pay later?"

She glares at me before walking away. I see August standing at the edge of my vision.

"You have to do this," I say, turning to him. His eyes are fixed on a spot on the ground. "This crown is the cure we've been looking for."

He raises his head. The tears have dried on his cheeks, leaving trails through the blood smears. His eyes are swollen from crying, but there's a small smile on his face. He doesn't speak, so I continue.

"I think we're going to be okay. Well, you're going to be okay, at least."

The next moment, his lips are slammed against mine, nearly knocking all the air from my lungs. I hardly have a second to relax before he presses his tongue to the seam of my lips. He tastes like blood and salt. My functioning arm reaches out and rests on his hip while his tangle around my neck. They settle there and pull me closer until we're chest to chest. I splay a hand against him, intending to push him away, but I leave it there, feeling his heart thud beneath my palm.

I'm addicted to him, which isn't good, knowing my brief history with substances.

But that doesn't stop me.

I can't imagine living in a world where he isn't by my side, and it's more than likely that I'll die with the memory of him on my lips. But that won't be enough to save us.

"You know when people say that something is the beginning of the end?" I say as I pull back, slipping my hand into his. Those unfallen tears run down my cheeks, but I don't brush them away.

He interlocks our fingers, squeezing my hand three times. On his other hand, he runs his thumb over the tip of his forefinger. "Yeah?"

"I think this is it."

Both of us pretend not to notice when Lilac's watch

starts to tick again. As the minute hand completes a full circle, the half-set sun moves.

We watch the sun fall beneath the horizon through teary eyes, painting the entire sky with shades of deep blue and purple. The colours will soon be consumed by the black despair of night, a symbol of suffering that tomorrow could bring.

I want to be grateful, but there will finally be a new day tomorrow.

All the pain we've suffered.

All the hurt we've felt.

Everything.

Gone.

But it won't be.

TWENTY

AUGUST

I wake up kneeling beside the bed I fell asleep in, hands clasped in a prayer, whatever magic the Forest used to keep us awake finally leaving my system. *Lilac's* magic, I realise. Even in my dreams, my stepmother haunts me, God taunts me, and I wonder if there can truly be any good in someone who created something like me. A fraud. A liar. An imposter.

Oliver lies beneath the sheets, his hair sprawled across the pillows, one hand curled up beside his face like a baby. He looks like his sister but in black and white: hair like the stars, skin like the moon. I count the steady rises and falls of his chest, each flicker of his eyelids as he dreams.

I count each of the lies I told him as I pull myself to my feet, but no reasonable explanation for my actions comes to mind. I just wanted to be special to him, to be the exact type of person he could love, to hide the parts of myself that I don't like until they became unrecognisable. Until I became someone new.

I shake my head to banish the thoughts, digging my nails into a bruise until the pain clears my mind. Oliver doesn't need to know. At least, not until I can summon the courage to leave him behind.

A mirror across the room catches my eye, the surface reflecting shades of red and blue that can't be seen in the world swathed in silver moonlight. I know the colours aren't real. I know I should resist pretending that they are. But there's an uncontrollable urge to believe that, just for a moment, I'm back in the place where I was before here, alive and at home and seeing things I did not quite understand.

I stand in front of the mirror and allow the colours to fill my vision until my face blurs into a resemblance of the person I used to be.

In my daydream, I'm sixteen and my best friend has just turned seventeen. It's New Year's Eve, and I've found out why the colours flicker across my vision and the shadowy figures in the corner of my eye don't fade away when I look at them. My dad cried when the doctor gave me a life expectancy. My stepmother examined her nails. My best friend smiled when they asked if I was okay, and I told them I was fine.

We're alone, sat together in the yellow-hued kitchen, me on the worktop and them leaning against it. We're drinking a pretty liquor with flakes of gold floating around in it that my father bought us as a treat, although only one of us has emptied their glass. We're both wearing party cracker paper crowns, and theirs crinkles against my skin as they kiss the palm of my hand with cinnamon lips. Strands of feathery brown hair tickle the inside of my wrist.

"I never had a best friend before I met you," I say, then let them press a sloppy kiss tasting of store-

275

brand vodka against my lips because that was what best friends did, wasn't it?

They say nothing back, but I wake up beside them the next morning with a new understanding that perhaps we were never only just friends, and it always felt right before, even if my stepmother told me it was wrong, and the church told me it was wrong, and the therapists told me it was wrong. It feels even more right that morning with the paper crowns screwed up on the floor and the taste of liquor still on my tongue.

It still feels right when my best friend returns home and I wake up the morning after that with a missed phone call and a voicemail that simply says, "We shouldn't have done that."

In my eyes, they could never do anything wrong; I took the people I loved and painted them in gold. Back then, I thought I was the thing that was wrong.

Now, I turn away from the mirror, blinking away the colours from my vision until my face blurs back into my current self. Fading bruises. Bitten lips. A crown soon to be stuck on my head, my own blood mingling with the blood dried across the surface, the blood of the previous child monarchs. It dawns on me that this is the face I will have forever if we can't find the gate: maybe eighteen, mostly dead, the eternal King of the Forest.

A flicker of light outside catches my attention, and I tiptoe towards the window, pressing my face against the stained glass until my breath turns cloudy. A figure that I make out to be Porcelain is crossing the courtyard, a lit torch held high, her scars glittering beneath the flame. She approaches two shadows: one tall and lithe and draped in a hooded cloak, the other shorter and holding a child-sized bundle that is almost as big as they are in their arms with ease. She greets the tall one with a deep bow and the other with a curt nod; something about their movements feels distantly familiar like I've met them in a memory.

Porcelain douses the torch, and the group talks in hushed voices in the moonlight, heads bowed together so I can't read their lips or their expressions. She taps her foot impatiently. The shorter figure shifts the bundle from arm to arm, and I'm convinced I can hear their joints creaking beneath the weight. The cloaked figure speaks with sweeping hand gestures, and I notice slender waxed white fingers and a sparkly silver brooch at their throat.

By the time their conversation ends, the sky is lightening, and they leave the way they came. Soon after they disappear into the shadows, two girls race into the courtyard from opposite sides and into each other's arms, a tall brunette and a waifish blonde. The brunette bends down so her lips brush the shell of the blonde's ear, her curls forming a curtain around the two of them. They are lovers, embracing in the quiet hours of the night, and I have to tear my gaze away from a moment that isn't mine to observe.

Instead, I look over my shoulder towards Oliver, stuck between feeling frozen and feeling everything. He's still sleeping, still dreaming. I wonder how long it'll take for him to clear me from his system if I leave right now before he realises I think of someone else when I kiss him, someone who I need to see one more time. Or that I'll never be able to love him the way I want to, not until I find a cure for my breaking heart. Not until my best friend is beside me in the trees.

Something inside me says that he'll understand if I tell him. He'll be patient, or he'll move on with someone else, but he'll accept me for who I am. But I don't want to wait and risk being wrong.

I slip back into the bed, tuck myself beneath one of his arms, and go back to pretending that I am someone other than myself.

TWENTY-ONE

The crowning ceremony takes place at sunrise. The sun has barely changed position in the sky by the time it's over, and the entire ceremony is underwhelming. We gather in the throne room—one of the few places that remained untouched after the battle—while a teenage boy dressed in a mock priest outfit reads from a scroll.

"We are gathered here today in recognition of the new leader of our Forest," the boy begins, his eyes flicking around the room, his expression otherwise vacant. I guess he was surrounded by more impressive company during the last coronation.

Two bodies are laid on pedestals behind him, covered with red velvet sheets. The former Queen. The girl who could have been a Queen. Both children. Both dead. August's eyes don't leave them for the duration of the ceremony.

The boy unravels the scroll further and splutters as a cloud of dust rises from it. "As soon as this crown is placed upon your head, you cannot remove it until the next leader is crowned. You will have power over anyone loyal to the previous leader and anyone loyal to you."

He reads out the rest of the known consequences of having the crown, not providing any more details than Porcelain did. August signs the bottom of the scroll with his blood, and it fizzles like a sparkler when it touches the parchment. Then he's rushed out of the room, on his way to meet with what remains of the older inhabitants of the Forest.

I'm left alone with Porcelain and a few stragglers. She's picking at the golden scars that mark her hands, some of them fresh.

"What are you going to do now?" I ask her.

She doesn't look at me. "All I can do is carry on as before. Many lives may have been lost, but there is still someone who holds the crown. That is all that matters to the Forest."

The boy with the scroll gasps dramatically, cutting our conversation short. When I turn to him, the room is filled with ghosts. They aren't the middle-aged ghosts dressed in suits and ballgowns that I grew up watching in films. There isn't a single adult standing among them. Instead, their ages range from toddlers to teenagers, all dressed casually in jeans and t-shirts with tears and fraying hems. A lot of them look just like me.

"What's going on?" I whisper to Porcelain. She acts unfazed by our newfound company, but their unblinking gazes make my heart rate double.

"They are the spirits of those who were harmed by the crown," she murmurs back, her lips barely moving. "They are vengeful spirits. They appear when the crown is passed from one leader to another so they can feed off the guilt to fuel their journey to the next afterlife."

"The guilt?"

"You can only receive the crown when the previous leader has died. In the Forest, the most common cause of death is murder, and many people have killed for the crown. That is something that people may feel guilty about."

I can't help but wonder if they're here for me, the boy who is used to mourning dead butterflies and dead sisters. But they're here for August, the one who brought Gracie here to die and allowed her to make the sacrifice. Neither of us did anything to stop it.

I turn to Porcelain again. "Do you feel guilty? Like, at all?"

Her expression turns to a scowl. "What do I have to feel guilty about?"

"You turned against a little girl who was supposed to be your friend. Your Queen. You shot her in the chest with your arrows. You encouraged everyone to hurt her. You didn't even shed a tear when you were standing over her dead body!"

"I do not have the time to feel guilty, and neither

do you." With that, she straightens the circlet beneath her hair and storms out of the room.

My gaze follows her as she leaves before returning to rest on the ghosts. I think I see my sister's face amongst them, and my heart becomes heavy at the realisation that it could've been the crown that killed her for the second time. The crown that is now stuck on August's head.

We watch each other across the room for a few moments. Brother and sister, no longer separated by death. Just like the first time I saw her ghost, her image flickers, and August appears where she stood.

"Where's Ansel?"

The courtyard is still covered with the bodies of fallen children waiting for burial as we leave the castle. The bodies are uncovered and unprepared for their final rest, and their skin is ashen and unwashed. The blood of the battle marks their clothing and congeals at the edges of their wounds. Many of their eyes remain open, as though accusing us of their cruel fate.

Some were still loyal to Lilac, but many were just desperate children who wanted to go back home, back to the lives that they had lost. Even if we find the gate, they won't be able to go back to their families. They'll never grow up to become the people they might have been. And, in this world, no one will even remember them. No one will mourn their loss. In days, or maybe even hours, they'll fade from everyone's memories.

Two older girls lift the first body—a boy, just younger than Ansel. Grabbing him by the shoulders and feet, they unceremoniously heave him away. Two smaller boys come for the next body. It's a girl with thick dark curls, barely older than me, and looking at her broken body sends waves of familiarity through me, but I'm too hurt to remember why. When the boys lift her roughly, a golden beige arm flops like the dead weight that it is. Part of it is missing, but there is no bloodied gash. It's just gone.

August and I stand and watch dozens of bodies being carried away, giving them names and stories like constellations. We don't know where they're going, but I wonder if they'll end up in the ravine like the person we found weeks ago. We stand there until it's Gracie's body that's being carried away, and it's suffocating to hold back my tears.

Ansel isn't laying in the courtyard with the other bodies. Instead, he's made his way into the trees, far enough away that he can't see the castle from any direction. By the time we get to him, the monster handprint on his arm has grown to cover most of his body, the skin bubbling like a blister.

"It hurts," he whimpers. He leans against a tree to support his weight, but his legs buckle beneath him. He takes another step before stumbling and falling to the ground. August remains by my side; even he knows there is no way to fix this. Dying is an incurable disease.

"You have to help him," he whispers, tugging at my sleeve.

I turn to look at him, trying not to look directly

into his eyes. "I don't have powers like Gracie. I can't heal him. I can't *fix* him."

"You can still help him." His hands drop to the dagger at his waist, unsheathing it and forcing it into my hand. "He's dying here, so he must be dying in the Otherworld. Make sure his family knows he didn't die in pain."

I can't promise that his death won't be painful, but I can make sure that his suffering doesn't drag out for much longer.

Ansel doesn't react when I walk towards him and kneel, only scratches at the still-growing burn spreading across his cheeks. Large sections of his skin peel like a sunburn, but a sunburn doesn't bleed.

"It hurts so bad." Bloody tears drip miserably down his face. "Please help me."

My hands fumble with the dagger and rest on the hilt. His eyes follow. I try not to think too much about what I must do. He does nothing to object to what happens next.

I bring the dagger up in an arc, the blade slamming

through his ribcage. I'm afraid that I've missed and put him in more pain, but the tip pierces his heart. The hilt of the blade protrudes from between his ribs.

Ansel gasps and spasms into my arms. His eyes are wide and, for a moment, I think I see shock and pain in them, and it hurts; it hurts somewhere deep down in a place I thought I had buried days ago, a place that thought he was a traitor to the rest of us.

"Oliver," he gasps again, starting to straighten, and now the look of pain in his eyes is fading and I see the beginning of peace. He gasps once more. His hands close around the hilt of the dagger, just above the wound. There isn't any blood.

With a scream of agony, he pulls the dagger free. The blood flows freely now, gushing down the sides of his body and across my hands. I look away, burying my face in my good arm. August's hand rests on my shoulder, but it doesn't provide me with any comfort. Ansel screams and screams and screams, and the sound is the same as it was when we were first attacked by the monsters.

The noise stops as suddenly as it started. Ansel still lies on his back in front of me. His skin has healed to look brand new. He turns his head towards me, his face white and tight like paper stretched over bone. He's still breathing.

I lean over him, urgency in my voice. "Ansel," I say. His eyes meet mine but they're vacant, almost as if he no longer recognises me. "Please. Tell me why you left us. Gracie wants…" I choke back a sob. "Gracie would've wanted to know."

His face crumples at the past tense. "I saw the drawing of the gate in the book." His voice is so quiet it's barely audible. My ear almost brushes his lips as I lean in closer. "I skipped back a few pages and read about the keys. I went to the castle. The man in the tower told me the riddle. You can only get the second key if you own the crown, so I challenged the girl for it. Now I'm here."

He takes a deep breath and his eyes flick up to the sky. They glaze over as if he's fallen into a dream.

"I think I need my glasses again."

Then he turns his face away, and his heart stops beating.

TWENTY-TWO

We cover Ansel's body in flowers. We place white violets and fireweed and bluebells until his skin is draped in a mosaic of petals. We stand beside him for a few minutes as if we're waiting for the other to speak, but neither of us can find the right words to say.

It begins to rain as we turn away. We walk in silence around the castle grounds until the day ebbs and the night slips across the sky in a sudden blanket, then August stops and turns to face me. "We're safe."

His wet hair becomes one with his face, tangled around the crown, draped over sharp features with sharper eyes. His expression is serious. "We're safe," he repeats firmly, and it sounds like he's trying to convince himself rather than me.

Slowly, I shake my head. "We're not safe until we've found that gate and key and got through to the other side and we're back home."

His face crumples for a second before he regains his composure. "Who's waiting for you at home?" He slips his arm through mine and we walk through the rain back to the castle.

"My mum and my stepdad, presuming they're still married. My little sisters—they're twins, Clara and Rose. One of them started ballet lessons a few months ago and was meant to have her first show around now. I promised her I'd be there, but I think I've missed it. I've got a baby brother too, even though he's not really a baby anymore. He hasn't been for years."

"Sounds like a lot of fun."

We laugh humourlessly, and I squint up at the stars through the rain clouds, searching for Riba. It seems as if there are a hundred more constellations than there were that day, and it reminds me that I am nothing more than a collection of atoms, insignificant in the grand scale of things.

"How long do you think we've been gone? My friends have probably forgotten about me by now. I was never a very present friend."

"It feels like months." August hesitates, unlinking our arms so he can trace circles on the back of his hand. "I hope everyone forgets about me. I want to start my life over. Being forgotten is the best thing this Forest will give me."

I stop walking and look at him. "Nobody wants to be forgotten."

He shrugs. "I like the idea of it. I like the idea that all the people who keep hurting me will just forget about me. Maybe my family will still remember me but will forget about all the pain so we can start again."

I think about the blanket fort in my bedroom and my painting propped on the mantelpiece, all the signs that I'm meant to be alive, meant to be remembered. But I also think about being suspended in the starry world in the pool and the unfamiliar voice that held my hand and how it was the first time I felt calm since I watched my sister die, and Carolina promising she could give me everything I've ever wanted.

Maybe what I want is to stay in the Forest and still be remembered.

By the time my mind returns to the present, we're back inside the castle and I'm alone in the bedroom, a cool breeze through open doors suggesting that August is on the balcony. He's silhouetted against the stars, leaning with his elbows on the railing as he chews at his lips until they turn bloody, the cloak he's draped around his shoulders for warmth turning him into a piece of the night. I linger in the doorway and wonder what people would think if they saw us together: a modern boy in old-fashioned clothes, a boy with a band t-shirt and a bloodstained crown. Both are not quite dead, but neither are alive. I hold on to the thought for a moment longer.

"I won't forget you," August says, as if he can sense my presence. I step onto the balcony as he turns to face me. "Even if I want you to forget about me."

He clasps my left hand in his right hand and rests the other on my lower back. My arm in the splint hangs limply by my side. We start slow dancing. No music, just the sounds of the Forest at night. He leans his head into the crook of my neck, and I bury my face in his hair. Dancing chest to chest. Revolving slowly, eyes closed, heartbeat measure, nature's hum. It lasts the length of an old song, and then we stop and the world resumes. My heart stays there, just like that, until the sky streaks with the soft pink of sunrise.

"You told Gracie that you love me," he whispers, his forehead pressing into my shoulder.

I nod. This is love, as reluctant as we may be to admit it to each other, but there is no other word for it.

I feel him nod back, his grip tightening on my shirt as if he's afraid to let me go.

I could stay here in this moment for the rest of time.

But we need to get home.

When he steps away from me, something has changed. I look at him, and he looks at me, and I realise that we're not quite in the same place where we used to be. His eyes are angry. All other emotions evaporate from his face. His focus is somewhere behind me, as if I don't exist to him. The last time he looked like this was when we had just met. That was when we were all angry, just a group of children dumped in a world that none of us understood. The anger that is still inside of him feels like a knife lodged in my ribs.

Even in this state, he's beautiful, but he seems more wild than I am.

"You might want to get away from the Forest tonight." His body trembles as he rubs at new unbruised skin swathing up his arms like a watercolour, cold purple and blue rosebuds receding against a canvas of warm brown.

I reach out to take his hand again, but he pulls it away. I try to hide my hurt. "Why?"

He tugs the cloak tighter around his shoulders—black and blue, like his skin used to be—and sighs. "I'm going to burn it to the ground."

TWENTY-THREE

ugust leaves the castle at dawn, sending a messenger to announce his departure. His council comes to see him off, dressed in light cloaks and dark smiles. He doesn't say why he's leaving, but they still nod and bow at his every word. They don't seem worried about their new King leaving the castle one day into his reign. I watch them all with a careful eye, as if I can spot if any of them will become a traitor.

"Please stay safe," I whisper to August as he hugs me goodbye, brushing my lips against his, the lingering blood sticking us together for a second. He buries his face into my shoulder, and I wind his curls around my fingers. I take the time to memorise him: the stab of his cheekbone pressing into my arm, the rasp of his laugh, the coppery scent of his skin.

I trace the route through the Forest that we agreed upon across his back: head west and cross the river to keep a break between me and the fire, then follow the river upstream until it meets the lakebed with the island in the centre. My finger follows the bumps of the back of his ribcage, the curve of his spine, the sharpness of his shoulder blades as I remember his route, the opposite direction of mine.

"Stay safe," I whisper into his hair. "Please, for me."

August nods, then inhales deeply. "You told Gracie you love me," he says, his voice muffled by my shoulder. "You told her you loved me."

"I did. I *do*."

He takes a step back, and my hand lingers on his shoulder, rubbing the fabric of his cloak between my fingers like a comfort blanket. His face is streaked with tears, and he's bitten his lip into another bloody mess. "Why would you say something so selfish?"

I falter at the cold response. For a moment, I'm convinced that my heart stops beating and that the world stands still before my eyes, frozen in time. I let go of his arm and, in some sad sort of way, I feel like I'm letting go of him. Or the version of him I've invented for myself. "Why would you say something so mean?"

He says nothing, just stares past me, his tears dripping into his mouth.

"I must be a selfish person," I continue. "One of us has to be. Or were you just going to pretend that this is nothing?" I gesture between the two of us. "You have a fucked-up view of love if you think that this is selfish."

He winces as if I'm the one hurting him. I want to. I'm going to.

"Maybe it's for the best if everyone forgets about you."

Time starts to move again. He looks at me as if he doesn't recognise me anymore, as if he sees straight through me. Then he turns away without another word.

I wonder if I'll ever see him again.

I walk through the Forest alone, the taste of August's blood and the bitterness of our goodbye still on my tongue.

Originally, I thought I was alone on my journey. A few hours after stopping to eat some dried berries and nuts from the supplies stored in my knapsack, I realise that there is something—someone—travelling with me. I catch glimpses of them in the corner of my eye. They are around thirty feet away from me, slipping silently through the trees that are now completely smooth and towering above me as they did on my third day of being dead, entirely obscuring my follower's figure in the shadows.

I drop to my knees and swing the knapsack onto the ground in front of me. Pretending to be searching through the bag, I risk glancing up at random intervals, masking my eyes with my shaggy hair.

Nothing moves for the next five minutes—not me, not my shadow, and not my lifeless surroundings.

A sudden gust of wind appears, and the edge of white fabric is visible from behind a tree. I see a pale hand hurriedly smoothing it out of sight. They're closer than I was expecting, a lot closer. They're close enough for me to reach out and grab them.

I leap to my feet, swinging the knapsack over my shoulder. My shadow notices my movement and darts deeper into the trees. They're quick, even swathed in fabric, and have a head start. They're clearly familiar with their surroundings as they weave through the trees. They have an advantage: I'm carrying a heavy bag and can't navigate the Forest and have been dead longer than I can figure out. They have an advantage, but I'm too determined, too desperate, to let them go. There must be a reason for them to follow me.

I chase them through the untamed parts of the Forest, where the trails descend into mud from recent rain and thick trees grow to cover them in archways. I chase them as I slip across uneven ground and twist my ankles on protruding tree roots. I chase them until my lungs burn and I'm gasping for one more breath.

Then I realise that I'm seeing the world through them.

With my last burst of energy, I reach out and grab the smoke girl, expecting my fingers to pass straight through her, but she becomes solid beneath my grip.

TWENTY-FOUR
AUGUST

I leave the castle at dawn, hands shaking, heart breaking, but I did what needed to be done.

Well, I let everyone think I leave. Instead, I walk through the trees until I am out of sight, then loop back and enter the castle through what could have been a servant's entrance in a past life. I summon the memories of what Oliver said about the castle and follow his directions towards the eastern turret, gasping for breath as I climb the stairs, fumbling with a key to enter the room at the top.

The Toyman is waiting for me on the other side of the door, silhouetted by candlelight. He wears a

309

patchwork cloak and a crumbling top hat that are both coated in thick dust. His mechanical eye scans me from head to toe while the real one watches me intently. The cogs in his chest sputter as if the magic that keeps him alive is running out. I wonder if he'll be here the next time someone enters this room.

"I don't belong here." I whisper, but my breath still unsettles the dust in the air. "This place is not my home."

The Toyman takes a step towards me, observing my face in the flickering light. "I told your friend what it will take to leave the Forest." He scowls as if he's had this conversation a hundred times before. "I will not tell you anything different."

I scowl back at him, tapping my thumb across my fingertips to keep myself calm. "We solved your riddle. We stole the crown. We have a key. We don't know how to find the other. We don't know where the gate is, so we can't get home."

There's a moment where neither of us speaks, just listen to the whirring of his heart and watch the dust settle. I wonder if coming here was a good idea. I should've told Oliver why I suddenly needed to leave and hoped that he would still love me. But I kept him in the dark and broke his heart.

Eventually, the Toyman raises what's left of one of his eyebrows. "How about a deal? A trade, if you would prefer. A bad memory for a good one. A moment from your past for a moment in your future."

A trade. *Oliver's* trade. My bad year in exchange for his butterflies. I can barely remember it anymore, only a pine tree and soft hands and softer lips.

I wonder if there are any more bad memories that I'm willing to surrender.

I wonder if there's a moment that I only want to relive once more.

There's one.

I turn to the Toyman and, with the most confidence I've felt since arriving in the Forest, I say, "I accept your trade."

In my daydream—my bad memory, if you'd prefer—I'm still sixteen, and it's a few weeks after New Year's Eve in the yellow-hued kitchen.

I was in that kitchen when I realised I wasn't in love with my best friend anymore, if I ever was. I could see it in the way they looked at me that night, colder than before, but warm enough to fool me one more time. But my best friend still sent me drunken texts at four in the morning for all the nights afterwards because they knew I would still be awake, staring at the ceiling until the sky turned light. After all, I couldn't sleep knowing that I could've done something to turn them away from me. I'd ignore the texts, but I answered the one phone call where no one said a word, and we listened to each other breathe for a few minutes until they hung up. I wanted to say that I missed them, that I still loved them. I wanted them to say the same.

A few months later, I still thought about them too much and did too little to get them out of my head, because I was still the same mess of a dreamer I was when I was a child finding stories in the stars. I wondered if they thought about me as much as I thought about them. I wondered what would have happened if I wished for a different person when I blew out the candles last year. I wondered if I was infected by their Ritalin smile.

I was still thinking about that smile later in the year when I was freshly seventeen and dying alone in a hospital bed, counting my last breaths like counting stars, spinning my mother's ring around my finger in a little ritual, choking down tears, choking out a prayer.

When I woke up in the Forest, I looked around for my best friend, the person I still loved more than the rest, desperate to catch one more glimpse of that smile, those eyes, their hair. The only way I could accept being in the afterlife would be if I brought them with me. And I couldn't accept that I was the one who had to die alone when they were the one who left me.

Outside of the daydream, I'm standing back in the trees, the Toyman by my side. We're knee-deep in water and surrounded by wiry trees that are propped up on a dense tangle of roots, high enough for me to stand beneath.

Beneath the roots of the nearest tree, there's a wrought-iron gate swinging in the tide, the air behind it pulsing like a current. A gate, but not the one in the book: it's too small, and there isn't a decorative piece on top. But there is a series of keyholes sunk into the closest root.

I trudge through the water for a closer look while the Toyman lingers behind me. "The gate? We only found one key."

I hear the amusement in his voice. "This one was opened during the rule of a former leader. It was wrong of Oliver to assume that Lilac created keys to unlock a gate. It was wrong of you to assume that only one gate would take you home."

"Was it wrong of us to trust you?"

He laughs, then coughs, then chokes. When I turn back towards him, the cogs in his chest seize with rust, as if bringing me here drained the last of his life force.

"It was wrong of you both to trust a strange person in a strange place. It was wrong of Porcelain to guide you to someone who stayed loyal to their Queen until both of their ends." One cog crumbles to dust. His metal eye moves erratically around the socket as if he's lost control of it. "And now you must decide if it is wrong for you to trust me one more time."

I look back at the gate. It feels too easy to have come all this way just to be handed the ending, to give up on the opportunity for a better life to return to my old one.

I look back towards the Toyman. Behind him, far enough away that the trees are oak and beech rather than mangroves, a plume of black smoke rises. There's a flicker of red and orange that isn't part of my imagination. Someone else has started the fire.

I look back and forth between the gate and the flames, then rub my knuckles into my eyes until my vision fills with colours. I think of the colours I first saw when my best friend blew out their birthday candles, making a wish that never came true.

Go home. Save myself.

Stay here. Save the Forest.

An orange butterfly lands on the edge of the gate. A monarch butterfly, wings barely moving, glowing candlelight. I think of trading memories and kisses and memories of kisses beside the brook.

Go home. Save myself.

Stay here. Save the children.

The Toyman coughs one more time and then falls silent. When I turn around, he is no longer there. All that remains is a dusty top hat sinking beneath the water. This decision doesn't belong to him.

Go home. Save myself.

Stay here. Save Oliver.

I take one more step towards the gate, ducking beneath the tree roots, startling the butterfly into flight. I look into the swirling air behind the gate and catch glimpses of a past life: the moonlit field, the suitcase on my bedroom floor, the yellow-hued kitchen. The memories are pulling me in.

Without another thought, I dip in my hand and think of home.

TWENTY-FIVE

"Who are you?"

The smoke girl doesn't try to pull away, just looks sadly down at my hand clasped around her arm. I remember my sister and her hand turning to mist as it drifted through me, too dead to touch. Then I realise that the smoke girl is solid beneath my grasp.

"Am I dead?" I ask the girl.

She smiles sadly. "We're all dead here."

I sink to the ground, stumbling against a large stone and uneven ground. A headstone. I'm sitting on someone's grave. The name is faded beyond recognition, but I pray for them anyway.

The smoke girl trails a ghostly finger across the top of another gravestone, flicking away strands of ivy that climb across the surface. Here, the Forest doesn't just rot through her—it rots around us. It's dense with trees, but they're decomposing and misshapen, stuck in a perpetual state of decay. The tree closest to me is soft with rot, its roots arthritic, its trunk split open and oozing what looks like black pus. A threadbare smattering of leaves still sprouts from its sagging branches, but they grow grey and mouldy and, when they fall, they land in the blighted ferns on the Forest floor. But the smoke girl doesn't seem to notice, continuing to play with the ivy.

"Who are you?" I ask again, my voice shaking. "Please."

Her voice is soft, as if it could be blown away by the breeze. "I was the first person in this Forest. In some ways, I think I made this place. First to live, first to die. I've been here so long that the name on my grave has faded. I think it's time for me to pick a new one." She drifts towards a blank gravestone, her eyes softening with fondness. I guess it's hers, the name truly vanished after existing for so long. "It's lonely being in a world where no one is alive, but you're still deader than all of them. May I tell you a story? One about this world."

I nod, and her hand grazes my cheek, and my vision is overwhelmed with her memories.

Once upon a time, a boy awoke in a strange place. His desires and his daydreams leaked into reality, and the people of this strange place decided to make him a King. Not the first, but far from the last.

He grew into an adult, found himself a wife, and they had two daughters: one fair, one dark. At first, he was a loving father, cherishing his daughters and treating them well. He was good to them and his wife until the eldest daughter turned twelve years old and the youngest was soon to be eight. He decided he needed a worthier heir to the throne. He wanted a King.

Without his wife knowing, he abandoned both of his daughters deep in the Forest, preferring no heir than a female one. He died of unnatural causes several years later, and his wife tracked down her daughters, knowing she too would die before finding a suitable monarch to rule the Forest.

The eldest daughter went willingly, becoming Queen, while the youngest fled deeper into the Forest. She didn't want to leave the man who raised them during their abandonment, the parent figure who cared for her unconditionally, but would rather leave him than return to the castle. The new Queen began stealing the hearts of her people, turning them into toys for her to play with, forcing them into obedience with artery blood still dripping down her arms. She wanted them to feel the same numbness in their chests that she felt when she was abandoned. She wanted to be powerful. And, above everything else, she wanted her own saviour, someone to take her to the world where her powers couldn't reach, where there was a whole new world for her to conquer.

Queen Carolina stole hearts and lives for a few more years until Lilac Bonneville appeared in the trees.

The smoke girl draws her hand away from my face, and the memories fade along with her touch.

But her memories don't match up with mine.

"It doesn't make sense," I tell her, trying to align our versions of the story.

Her hand freezes in the air. "It doesn't?"

"No." I pull myself to my feet, brushing dead leaves off my clothes. "The Toyman said that Carolina came from the Otherworld and can't return to her body. Your story said that she was born here. It doesn't make sense."

The smoke girl's hand drops to her side, tangling in the skirt of her dress. "Tales get twisted here," she begins hesitantly, as if she's letting me in on a secret that she isn't quite ready to share. "Tales depend on the teller. What they believe is the truth can become the truth, thanks to the magic in the air. True truth may become lost. Lies may become fact."

"What do you believe is true?"

"I believe Carolina was born here. I served on the court at the time of her birth. Some hearts she stole belonged to my friends. But you more than most should understand that the Forest has a way of manipulating your mind."

I turn this information over and over in my head until I can untangle the threads and something starts to make sense. I think about my memories that now have two different endings and my stories that now belong to someone else. I wonder if imagination and hope are enough to change the ending one more time.

For a moment, I accept she could be telling the truth.

I move on. "Why did she stop? Carolina, I mean."

"Oh, she hasn't stopped." Her eyes turned to stone as she laughed bitterly. She kneels and begins tracing a familiar image into the dirt: a large circle, a line splitting it in half and another line splitting one half into quarters. She adds the shapes that I've grown to recognise, and then an X outside of the circle, stabbing at the lines with a fingertip. "She went into hiding the moment someone more powerful than her appeared. She now works in private in a hidden factory, far past the borders of the Forest where the leader's powers can reach. All she left behind is a key."

That's when I consider that Carolina, monarch by birth, the true holder of the crown, may be who the Toyman was talking about in his riddle. And I missed my chance for Carolina to help me.

"I was a Queen once," the smoke girl says, drifting towards another worn gravestone. I wonder how long it's been since someone stopped to talk to her. "One of the first ones. Back before you had to kill to take the throne. The next leader kept me around because I still had powers without the crown. Then I still had powers without a body. They held on to me to be useful for them in case I went rogue." She smirks at the thought. "I spend my time looking for the other daughter. Our lost princess. I don't make it very far before someone calls me back, but I know I'll find her someday. We will."

I add the lost princess to the list of things I'll never solve about the Forest, closely followed by Carolina's army and the powers of the past monarchs. I wonder if it was Carolina who sent the metal soldiers to find us in the ravine rather than Lilac.

After a few moments of thought, the smoke girl reaches towards me and traces a finger along my forearm, her nail snagging on my sleeve as if she knows what she'll find beneath. The fabric slips up and I glimpse an ageing wound across my skin.

I pull up the sleeve to look at where I carved my own name into my arm. Instead of raised scar tissue, the cuts have sunk into my skin, a part of my flesh well and truly gone to leave me behind as a permanent reminder. Sometimes, a name is all you have to remember who you are.

The smoke girl nods as if she's approving. "Names are important. Names are powerful."

"Can I give you a new name?" I blurt. "Someone special to me still doesn't have a headstone. They were more expensive than we were expecting."

She nods enthusiastically, holding out her arm. I take her hand in mine—warm, lifelike—and navigate my splinted arm until I can trace familiar letters across her skin, the ones that adorned every birthday card and gift tag and handwritten made-up fairytale from the first seven years of my life. It's now that I realise that I've lived longer without her than with her.

ROWAN.

The surrounding air shivers silver as if the Forest has given its blessing. I hope my sister approves, too.

The smoke girl—Rowan—beams. She looks down at her arm as if I've left a permanent mark to mirror my own. "I will take care of this name for you, Oliver. You are a good soul." Then, after a pause, "I hope you find the way home."

When she starts to fade away, I see that the world through her is on fire.

TWENTY-SIX

The world does not end in a bang or a whisper, but one scream at a time.

First, it's the birds, once silent, now screeching as sparks burn their wings and the ancient trees groan and send their nests crashing to the ground. I swat at a burning feather that falls too close for comfort.

Next, it's a mud-covered girl who must've been hiding out in the trees since she arrived in the Forest. She runs as fast as she can, stumbling over roots and rocks as she passes me without a second glance. A flaming branch falls and crushes her against the ground in a shower of sparks. Her screaming stops.

After that, it's me, yelling as fiery embers drop onto my skin, my clothing doing nothing to protect me from the inferno. I try to reorientate myself, to work out where I was before I followed Rowan to the graveyard, to find the river that was supposed to be the river between me and the fire. But it's no use, not with the air filling with black smoke and burning branches blocking the paths. I abandon the paths and run, cursing August's name with each breath, wishing he stayed with each step.

The world has transformed into one of smoke and flame. I try to follow a wild creature through the trees, trusting its instincts to be sharper than mine, but it flies through the underbrush too fast for me to keep up with. Instead, I keep running in that direction, my boots catching on roots and fallen branches. The smoke threatens to suffocate me at any moment as I gasp for breath, running, choking, my face cut with twigs that appear from the black haze without warning.

Then, I hear something. It's quiet, but I can hear

running water beneath the roar of the fire. I picked the right path after all.

After a few more frantic strides, the river materialises through the trees. It's wide enough that I can't see the other side with the amount of smoke in the air. But I know it'll only take a few more steps for me to reach the river and swim to safety.

Something stops me.

A tree tries to run from the flames. A living tree, foul and twisted, covered in moss and rotting vines, tugging its roots from the ground as it attempts to escape. It has branches instead of bone, matted with leaves and dirt rather than blood and flesh. Dark, panicked eyes peer out of the wild undergrowth that covers its face. Sickly yellow sap runs down from its eyes, mimicking the path of tears. It groans like a whale song as it struggles to free itself.

I want to help it, but I'm becoming dizzy from the smoke. A cough racks through my body, and my lungs constrict as if they're being cooked. Each breath sends a searing pain in my chest until discomfort turns to distress.

Keep running. Save myself.

Stop running. Save the creature.

I have no doubts.

I run towards the creature and drop to my knees at its feet, clawing at the dirt that traps its roots, careful to avoid touching or hurting it. I dig with my hands until my nails crack and my injured arm breaks further from the effort and my fingertips turn bloody. Removing the dirt frees most of the roots, but there's one tucked too deep into the soil to rescue without damage. I tear it free and send a sticky black sap spurting across my hands, yelling an apology to the creature as if we speak the same language. It gurgles in what I decide is gratitude and then splashes into the river, following the current downstream.

When it's drifted out of sight, I stumble into the water. It's not deep enough to swim, and the current is almost strong enough to sweep me away. But I focus on the far side as if I can see it through the smoky haze, brow furrowed, determined to take step after step and not slip. Step after step until I reach the other side and collapse onto the bank.

As I pause to catch my breath, I realise that this isn't the safe side of the river: this side has already burnt to the ground. The Forest that was once so alive now chills me. Embers from the fire still burn red, and fingers of smoke creep towards me, but my body shakes from an imagined chill. The trees that sheltered with their deep green canopy are now lifeless stumps of charcoal. The unconstrained daylight illuminates the scorched ground, and the earthy smell that I woke up to all that time ago still lingers, despite the burning behind me.

If I close my eyes, I will still see the perpetual orange mosaic above, the warm breeze on my skin, the sound of birdsongs that I'll never recognise. I will still see August's face, glowing golden in the light of the half-set sun, smouldering amber against the campfire we kissed in front of. I want to wonder if he survived his fire, if this is what he wanted to happen. But I won't. I can't. Not after he chose to break my heart.

Now, there's nothing left for me to do but keep moving until I find a place that is untouched by the fire. To start over. Everything is wood, so everything is burned, and everything that I grew to love is gone. Soon, the air will be too smoky to breathe and hot enough to scorch my skin without even having to touch the flames.

When the words do not come, the tears do. I was raised to believe that mourning should be dignified—we were scolded for weeping at my sister's funeral—but now I bawl like a child with running snot and choking sobs, and I'm not ashamed. I sink to my knees, not caring about the embers that burn and blister my body.

I cry until there is nothing left inside but raw emptiness. My eyeballs hang heavy in their sockets and my body hangs limp like each limb weighs twice as much as it had before. Moving is a slow, painful effort. The sun starts to shine in the sky, but not for me. The birds start to sing in bursts of melody, but not for me. The weather turns to a fine rain and leaves scatters of a rainbow behind, but not for me. For me, there is no beauty left in this world, no fresh start, no second chance. There's nothing here worth staying for.

When I look up, I notice that the grass has started

to regrow, a vibrant green patch that only covers the areas I've touched. A few flowers sprout up between my fingertips and their orange glow isn't just from the embers.

The Forest may regrow, but it won't bring my last chance at life back to me.

It won't bring August or my sister back to me.

It won't get me home.

EPILOGUE

U sually, in a counselling room with a circle of chairs, you would expect to find a group of teenagers. They would have empty eyes and slumped postures and minds that told them they were immune to the influence of society. However, those influences would be the reason they were in that room in the first place.

Now, the room is full of adults, holding on to each other as their final shreds of hope fade away, the flickering candle blowing out.

"We'll go around the circle one by one," says a man who stands at the edge of the circle, scratching at the stubble across his cheeks. "Introduce yourself and tell us a little about why you're here, as much as you're comfortable sharing. Remember, we're here to support each other, not to block each other out."

The first person to stand is a woman, likely to be in her late forties or early fifties but looking many years past her age. She has the delicate features of a porcelain doll, but her tears smear her carefully applied makeup and her skin looks many sizes too big for her skinny frame. She's wearing the same clothes as she was the last time she was here. There's a man beside her with an untrimmed moustache and a fuller figure from comfort eating. He doesn't stand.

"I'm Caroline Harwood. This is my husband, Michael. Our son...*My* son...His name is Oliver. He's still in a coma. It's his eighteenth birthday today."

Her hands no longer shake as she talks, but her voice falters. Her words sound rehearsed, almost as if she's been repeating the same story over and over again to other counsellors, private therapists, or old friends who come for visits and ask where her eldest son is that day. The man beside her resists the urge to reach up and hold one of her hands in both of his own.

"He overdosed on heroin…It must be two months ago now. The doctors know that his condition has suddenly taken a turn for the worse. He's still on life support. I'm praying for the best, but we're talking about switching it off."

A few tears leak out of her eyes as she sinks back into her chair, not uttering another word for the rest of the session.

The counsellor continues around the circle, all wet cheeks and hollow eyes blurring into one figure, looking like despair has been personified.

A young man is representing a little girl named Gracie. A woman in a wheelchair sits beside him and he rests a hand on her shoulder in comfort. Their daughter was left critically injured at age seven in a car accident where the man was driving. She died in the hospital earlier in the week. An elderly couple speaks about their grandson, Ansel, only fourteen years old. His death was more sudden: they truly believed that he was going to make it.

A middle-aged man is here to talk about his son, August. The woman isn't with him. On his left hand, where the fourth finger meets the knuckle, there's a ring of skin that is pasty white rather than tanned like the rest of his body.

"I thought my son was a terminal cancer patient and that any day would be his last. By some kind of miracle, he's improving. The tumour has started responding to the treatment."

He smiles, but it isn't directed at anyone in the circle. The adults turn around and see a teenage boy standing in the shadows of the doorway. Even in the darkness, his eyes are Atlantic blue. One of them is framed by a fading bruise. He smiles back and there's no sign of sadness on his face.

The counsellor smiles too, but it doesn't reach his eyes. "One thing that you all have in common is that you have a child who is on the verge of being taken away from you, whether it is by a natural illness or something that could've been prevented. You mustn't worry, for they have been placed in the best hands and there are people who are trying their best to look after them."

The adults in the circle lean in, desperate to hear anything that could ease their pain, even if it's just a story woven for their own comfort. In this situation, it is a story, although there is some truth behind every word.

"While your children and grandchildren are away, I like to think that they're visiting a fantastic place, somewhere where they aren't restrained by an illness or held back by their own emotions. I like to believe that they're in a place called the Paper Forest, where there is nothing but health and happiness to greet them."

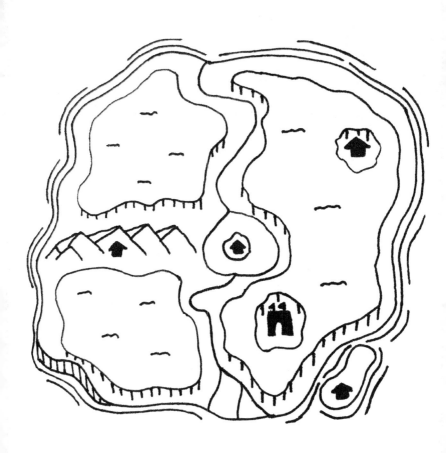

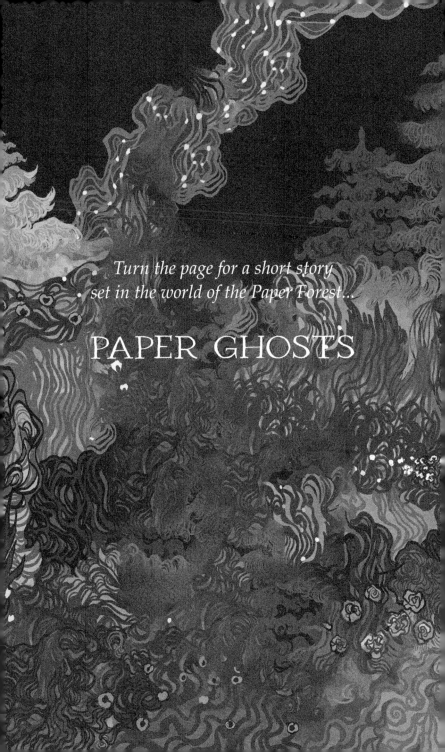

*Turn the page for a short story
set in the world of the Paper Forest...*

PAPER GHOSTS

ROWAN

The morning after the next King is crowned, the Forest burns to the ground, embers and ashes coating the kingdom in an ocean of black. The sun is blocked out by a smoky grey haze and all sounds are muffled by a blanket of soot. For a moment, there is peace in the Forest.

Rowan sits in the shadow of the skeletal remains of an oak tree, watching Oliver as he cradles a smouldering leaf against his chest as if he can make it alive again, as if he has the power to do something like that. He doesn't. But neither does the Forest, not anymore; it will take more than a lifetime for this area to recover from the flames. Rowan can taste the untamed magic in the air, the rusty tang that accompanies the power from the crown, and she knows the King wanted this to happen and that the Forest will do nothing but obey. Fortunately, he could not spread his dead spot any further than the places that he'd been, leaving it as only a pinprick-sized blight on the map.

What remains in the atmosphere is like a sickness, clinging onto the magic inside Rowan and tearing it out of her bloodstream, trying to find a cure for the disease of death. She wants to leave—*needs* to leave—before what is left of her drains away, but she won't. She won't leave Oliver alone while the Forest is also sinking its claws into him.

She watches him—his loss, his innocence, his humanity—and wonders if he'll ever move. He could stay here forever if he wanted to, but it wouldn't be wise. The fire ravaged the Forest, burning magic, blurring memories, and it will only be a matter of time until it starts scratching at his soul to recover, consuming the magic of his first memory, absorbing the moment of his last. He won't notice that something is missing until it is too late, until the only thing he can remember is the thing right in front of him.

Rowan thinks that the afterlife would be easier for most people that way: why would you want to be forgotten when you can just forget? But she knows she clings to her final fragmented memories of her past life like a life raft. They are the only things she has left that make her feel like she's real.

She thinks of her family infrequently but fondly, always pushing away the oddness in her gut that she gets any time she remembers that her younger sister isn't four anymore. She has aged beyond her older sister, and while the maths remains impossible to comprehend, it is an old wound by now. She knows that any person who once knew her name has been dead for a long time. How real are you if no one thinks about you, no one remembers you?

She's not sure if she remembers her sister's name anymore. She is sure that she doesn't remember her face, just another blurry spot in the fading photograph of her memories, an incomplete stranger if she ever arrived in the Forest.

Rowan watches Oliver some more as a distraction, bathing in his grief, missing when she still had someone to miss. She wasn't always the ghost of a girl trapped under someone else's command. Once upon a time, back in the early days of the Forest, she was the one in command, and this kingdom bowed down to her. She dismisses the fleeting thoughts with a sharp shake of her head; she's lived too many lifetimes to keep clinging to her first one.

But Oliver is still in his first lifetime, and he's spending it wasting away in the dead spot. One day, if he decides he wants to stay in the Forest, Rowan will teach him how to spot the stray magic in the air, how to see through spells, see through shadows, but for now she allows him to mourn his past self. An afterlife is still a life.

At least she thinks it is.

Rowan watches Oliver until his hands are still and he slips into sleep, then she feels a familiar tug in her chest: she is being summoned to the castle. Someone needs the help of one of the few powerful people left in the Forest.

With a sigh, she tears her gaze away from the sleeping boy and instead focuses on the shadow of the oak tree, prodding and poking with her power until the surface opens wide enough for her to slip into. The initial entry used to hurt at first, electricity breaking apart her atoms one by one and then stitching them back together on the other side, but she's learned to tolerate the pain of being torn apart over and over again. She used to wonder if a piece of her had been left behind during the journey, if the Forest had taken a souvenir from her travels, but then she learned about the misplaced magic in the dead spots and decided that it was her mind being stolen rather than her physical form.

With one last glance at Oliver, Rowan finds a gap in the seam between places, and the darkness swallows her whole.

When Rowan slips out the other side of the shadow, she finds the castle in turmoil. The air in the throne room is thick with smoke, and tendrils of flames creep through a window and wrap around a velvet curtain. The translucent maps that were hung on either side of the grand doors have disintegrated to ash. A girl tears down a tapestry that was made by an earlier Queen's court and tries to fan some of the smoke out of the room. It does nothing to scare off the fire that is still burning bright.

There's a heap of bodies piled in front of the empty throne, charred from where they were caught outside in the presumed safety of the courtyard when the fire began. Beside them, a living boy curls in on himself, his body shaking as he chokes up black tar, but doesn't have the strength to spit it out. Rowan is the only one to notice when the rise and fall of his chest suddenly stills. She gasps out a prayer for him.

It's a shame to see so much loss at once, to see the Forest taking lives much faster than they once would've returned, but the population will heal. Something has been happening at home to bring more visitors into the trees than before. Until the next group finds their way to the castle, Rowan will keep the deceased's memories safe, remembering them in her graveyard until they don't need her anymore.

Porcelain spots Rowan across the room. "You!" she snarls, her golden scars blazing in the firelight, her amber eyes burning just the same. She marches towards the ghost girl, abandoning the fight against the flames and shoving aside anyone who crosses her path. "You were told to keep track of the boy. Where did he go? How did he do this?"

Rowan decides that her lack of a physical body is the only thing stopping Porcelain from grabbing her by the collar and shaking her. She shrugs, for she was keeping track of Oliver instead, the one who the Forest was more interested in than the King. Maybe that was a mistake. People came, and people left the Forest all the time, arriving in fours, leaving alone, but the crown had rarely left the confines of the castle. Why would you want to leave when you have an entire afterlife to play God with near-infinite power?

But the King found his way home and is still playing God.

Rowan considers the consequences of this. So far, any part of the Forest within a handful of miles from the castle has burnt to the ground. A dozen people have died inside the castle, and countless more have died outside of the walls. No one will ever know how many Forest creatures or species of magical wildlife have perished. Other than that, the damage is barely worse than many of the monarchs' last days of life.

"You must find the boy." Porcelain's voice drags Rowan's attention back to reality. She notes the lack of a name or title. "The Forest will not survive without him. We will not survive without him."

Rowan wonders if she can survive if she's already died twice. In some ways, dying should make you exempt from death. She doesn't think that Porcelain will appreciate the thought, so she keeps it to herself. She also doesn't think that Porcelain will appreciate her pointing out that they already know where the King is and that he is somewhere completely unreachable to them unless he returns by choice.

Unless someone living leaves to bring him back without a choice.

They stand in silent disagreement until the sound of the ceiling crumbling captures Porcelain's attention, and then Rowan uses the distraction to slip away, focusing on the darkness between the cracks in the stone floor. There's a moment where she misses how Gracie's fear of monsters lurking in the dark halted time and the Forest was cast in endless shadows and infinite half-light for her to slip into. She wonders if another powerful child will arrive before the King returns, if they'll follow in the footsteps of previous monarchs and usurp the crown, swearing Rowan back into an existence of servitude. The monarch escaping the Forest is uncharted waters, and she's intrigued by all the possibilities, the opportunities, the temporary freedom. She's excited to exist as herself for just a moment in time.

Rowan emerges from the other side of the shadow in a quiet corridor far from the throne room, a place frozen in time where footprints haven't unsettled the dust in many reigns. Once, her footsteps marked these floorboards, leading the way to the sprawling series of rooms that were reserved for the early monarchs. She built those rooms for herself, but now she's just a ghost in her own home.

She wills herself to become as solid as possible so she can feel the gnarled wood beneath her bare feet, swiping the dust away until the corridor almost has the illusion of being lived in, tugging back the moulding curtains until flickering firelight can stream through the cracked windowpanes. She enters her old bedroom by turning the doorknob instead of slipping through the darkness of the keyhole—no one thought that the room was worth locking—and shuts it softly behind her as if someone could be listening. She presses her back against the door before sinking to the floor, tucking her knees under her chin and breathing a sigh of relief into the silence.

She's home.

The room is as she left it.

The dip in the mattress that matches the shape of

her body and the dent in the pillow that outlines the delicate angles of her face.

The charcoal drawings on loose parchment sprawled across the desk that weren't drawn by her hand, but she once treasured every single blackened stroke as if they were.

The nail missing from the loose floorboard and the nail that was only hammered in halfway, a scrap of torn fabric from an old sunflower yellow dress still caught around it.

The loose floorboard.

In the space beneath, she hid a personal history of the Forest, dozens of handmade and handwritten books documenting every moment from her first day to one of her last, until the author packed all that she couldn't hide away and left the castle for good.

They're still there.

Rowan pulls out the closest of the books, cradling it against her chest like an infant for a moment before turning to the first page. Familiar handwriting floods the page, looping vowels and sprawling consonants, pools of dried ink where the author held his pen against the paper in thought and T's crossed enough to cover the whole word. It is one of the later books—the craftsmanship of the book itself is too well-polished compared to early versions—but the text references a moment from their first month in the Forest, one that Rowan had almost forgotten about. She gasps at the familiarity of the moment, and then her head swims as her vision fills with a memory.

The Forest was peaceful on the twenty-seventh day. The occupants were four: Rowan, Isaac, Wesley, and Imogene. Rowan was the youngest, only seven when she met death, but she grew into her power effortlessly without questioning her newfound abilities.

Isaac fashioned a journal out of leaves and documented everything in the ashes of charred twigs from the fire, from the extent of Rowan's powers to theories about how to return to their families. Wesley hung from the branches until they broke and built shelters and fences around the area of the Forest that they now called 'home'. Imogene watched with a combination of awe and envy as Rowan manipulated the branches into planks and the shelters into a wood cabin, rooms adding and expanding with only a thought.

They all helped to craft Rowan a crown of ivy, and she made a pear tree bloom so they could eat the fruit. One day, she bloomed bushes without realising that the berries were poisonous, and then the occupants were three.

The ivy crown changed that day, the leaves darkening with rot and the vines growing bristles as if they could sense the death, as if it was intentional and there was a darkness brewing inside of Rowan. They brushed it off as a sign of natural decay rather than a sign of the Forest caring about what they did while residing in it.

But those three occupants were the first conscious beings that the Forest had ever seen, and it was excited to exist with something else that was alive. It had no mouth, no hands, no body at the time, so it could only communicate by sending sign after sign until it wasn't ignored anymore.

The Forest was no longer peaceful by the eighty-ninth day. Another group of four arrived, their names not important enough for Rowan to remember, but they came with another powerful child, a boy this time. The first three considered them dangerous, forcing the four to bow to the crown that grew blackened thorns and tied them to trees until Rowan's power learned to make iron bars and windowless rooms beneath the beginnings of a castle. The powerless ones were released soon after her second death and the population had grown enough that none of them recognised her face anymore.

After that first imprisonment, the three passed around the crown like kids playing pretend, taking turns to be the monarch and rule over their paper kingdom, much to the Forest's disdain. The Forest liked rules, liked consistency, liked order, and the lack of leaders and laws defied that. The three made up rules as they saw fit, changed them when they grew bored, and tricked people into breaking them for entertainment. Soon, the cells were full, and any further wrongdoers were exiled into the trees that had begun to house monsters. A girl broke Wesley's neck and stole the crown—looking more iron than ivy by now—after her girlfriend was sent into the Forest, and then what remained of the first four occupants became two.

Rowan knows that the first boy is still in the dungeons after all these years: she can feel the stab of his magic when she's close, still feel the barbed wire of his anger twisting around her chest. One day, she'll be brave enough to tell someone the reason he's down there or to free him herself, but she knows he's grown stronger. The years alone were also years to hone his power, and she fears she has created the next monster.

She's only just watched one monster be defeated. She's not ready to help conquer another.

Rowan's concentration slips for a fraction of a heartbeat, and she becomes unsolid once more, the book falling to the floor and breaking her out of the memory. She had forgotten about those days long enough to forget why she wanted to. She decides she is going to try to forget them again for a while longer, until she's strong enough to go back and fix her past mistakes. Until then, the boy stays in the dungeon, and her castle and crown remain a prison of her own design.

Maybe it isn't the monarch that is holding Rowan hostage.

Maybe it's just her.

Rowan's shadow takes her to a place alongside the river, just on the border of the dead spot. She floats across the surface of the water and sinks into the ashes on the other side, glad that they can't stain her clothes or stick to her skin anymore, sad that she can't feel the current against her feet. As she steps deeper into the dead spot, she can smell incoming rain—not the scent of rainfall, but the writhing odour of another storm brewing, the smell of air moving through water. She wonders if this is also one of the King's wishes, quelling the fire that he started, a sign of regret for his destruction, but she pushes the thought away. It's unlike a monarch of the Forest to show remorse.

Oliver is in the same place she left him, looking like a boy who could be a ghost himself, his skin deathly white and his cheeks streaked with soot. He's not sleeping anymore. Instead, he's kneeling in the ashes, his hands grasping at the ground beneath, breathing shallowly as he ignores the burn of embers. The remains of the smouldering leaf rest in his lap.

Rowan shows a phantom of a smile, in awe of his naïve humanity and his commitment to bringing life back to this area of the Forest when the evidence of his failure lies in his lap. But, after a breath, there's a familiar golden spark beneath the ashes, and she can taste blood in the back of her throat.

Between Oliver's fingers, a vibrant green tuft of grass sprouts up, orange daisies twisting around his fingertips. They wrap around his knuckles and his wrists and spiral up his arms until they curl around his head like a crown. The remains of the leaf stitch themselves back together until Rowan can see that it fell from an oak tree.

She feels a murmur in the air, a brush of magic

that is not meant for her to hear.

Save me, the Forest whispers to Oliver.

He flinches at the presence of the voice, frantically looking around for the source.

Save me, the Forest whispers again, a little louder this time, a little braver.

"What do you want from me?" Oliver asks, his voice barely louder than the first whisper.

There's a moment of quiet, and Rowan watches his brow furrow as if he's hearing the voice inside his head. He squeezes his eyes shut as if it hurts. She wishes the Forest treasured her enough to speak to her like that, not painfully, but directly, almost like an equal.

Save me, the Forest whispers aloud one final time. *Help me. Heal me.*

Oliver rubs the oak leaf between his fingers like a child with a comfort blanket, then squints up at the sky as if he's looking for a god. He mutters something to himself. Rowan wonders if it's a prayer. Finally, he nods.

Once.

"I'll do it."

Time seems to stand still for a moment. Ashes stay suspended in the air. A cloud pauses in front of the sun. Rowan's breath sticks in her throat.

Then, the Forest smiles. The sun starts to shine in the sky, burning away any signs of the incoming storm, replacing the clouds with scatters of a rainbow. The birds start to sing in bursts of melody, a fanfare to a new kingdom. The flowers of Oliver's crown glow golden and the petals twitch in dance. He laughs—just for a moment, almost as if he stops when he notices—and it's the most joyous sound that Rowan has ever heard.

The Forest smiles because, after all, there's nothing the Forest wants more than a King.

ACKNOWLEDGEMENTS

I have been making books since I was fifteen but I've somehow managed to avoid writing acknowledgements all these years. So, here is my very overdue gratitude to all of the people who made this book possible, from the first draft to the final copy.

Here we go.

To the Movellas community, who were the first people to read this book back when I was drafting it and uploading unedited chapters as soon as I finished writing them. And to the people who voted an early version of *Paper Forests* as 'Movella of the Year' in 2017. I have been riding that high ever since.

To Emma, my big sister across the ocean, for having no clue what I was writing but recognising that it was important to me, and giving her unconditional love and support nevertheless. And for finally freeing this book of typos.

To Han, my platonic soulmate and unintentional co-founder of Little Oaks Independent Publishing, this book would never have been finished without Glee binges and the bardcore playlists.

To Miss Lane, my secondary school English teacher, whose postcard expressing excitement for my second book has lived on my desk and encouraged me to keep writing for the past five years.

To you, for reading my books, for watching my videos, for cheering me on from Pinterest boards to unedited first drafts to final copies. This support will always mean more to me than I have the words to describe.

This book is a love letter to my dreams: to fish-shaped constellations, fairytales with unhappy endings, and soft boys with bloody knuckles. It's a love letter to the child in my memories who is still made of magic and monsters and would read fairytales under a chestnut tree. And, most of all, this book is a love letter to the Forest.

ABOUT THE AUTHOR

On a cold Autumn evening back in 2008, seven-year-old Tegan Anderson began to write their first short stories, finding a more creative way to learn their spellings. Many years and many more short stories later, they haven't stopped for anything. Now, they're writing more than they ever believed possible.

Tegan may write the worlds they would prefer to exist in but currently lives in Devon with their overflowing bookshelves and expanding imagination.

Printed in Great Britain
by Amazon